Washington Irving (April 3, 1783 – November 28, 1859) was an American short-story writer, essayist, biographer, historian, and diplomat of the early 19th century. He is best known for his short stories "Rip Van Winkle" (1819) and "The Legend of Sleepy Hollow" (1820), both of which appear in his collection The Sketch Book of Geoffrey Crayon, Gent. His historical works include biographies of Oliver Goldsmith, Muhammad and George Washington, as well as several histories of 15th-century Spain that deal with subjects such as Alhambra, Christopher Columbus and the Moors. Irving served as American ambassador to Spain in the 1840s.

Washington Irving

RIP VAN WINKLE

AND OTHER WRITINGS

DELHI OPEN BOOKS

RIP VAN WINKLE AND OTHER WRITINGS
by WASHINGTON IRVING

Edition copyright © Delhi Open Books, 2022

Published by

DⓘB

Delhi Open Books

G/F, 4771/23, Bharat Ram Road, Daryaganj, New Delhi-110002
Ph.: 91-11-42408081
E-mail: **delhiopenbooks2016@gmail.com**

ISBN: 978-93-95346-73-3

Cover, Typesetting, and Book Design by **ROHIT**

Contents

A POSTHUMOUS WRITING OF DIEDRICH KNICKERBOCKER

By Wooden, God of Saxons,

From whence comes Wednesday, that is Wednesday,

Truth is a thing that ever I will keep

Unto thylke day in which I creep into My sepulchre.

CARTWRIGHT

The following Tale was found among the papers of the late Diedrich Knickerbocker, an old gentleman of New York, who was very curious in the Dutch history of the province, and the manners of the descendants from its primitive settlers. His historical researches, however, did not lie so much among books as among men; for the former are lamentably scanty on his favourite topics; whereas he found the old burghers, and still more their wives, rich in that legendary lore, so invaluable to true history. Whenever, therefore, he happened upon a genuine Dutch family, snugly shut up in its low-roofed farmhouse, under a spreading sycamore, he looked upon it as a little clasped volume of black-letter, and studied it with the zeal of a book-worm.

The result of all these researches was a history of the province during the reign of the Dutch governors, which he published some years since. There have been various opinions as to the literary character of his work, and, to tell the truth, it is not a whit better than it should be. Its chief merit is its scrupulous accuracy, which indeed was a little questioned on its first appearance, but has since been completely established;

and it is now admitted into all historical collections, as a book of unquestionable authority.

The old gentleman died shortly after the publication of his work, and now that he is dead and gone, it cannot do much harm to his memory to say that his time might have been better employed in weightier labours. He, however, was apt to ride his hobby his own way; and though it did now and then kick up the dust a little in the eyes of his neighbours, and grieve the spirit of some friends, for whom he felt the truest deference and affection; yet his errors and follies are remembered "more in sorrow than in anger," and it begins to be suspected, that he never intended to injure or offend. But however, his memory may be appreciated by critics, it is still held dear by many folks, whose good opinion is well worth having; particularly by certain biscuit-bakers, who have gone so far as to imprint his likeness on their new-year cakes; and have thus given him a chance for immortality, almost equal to the being stamped on a Waterloo Medal, or a Queen Anne's Farthing.

***

Whoever has made a voyage up the Hudson must remember the Catskill mountains. They are a dismembered branch of the great Appalachian family, and are seen away to the west of the river, swelling up to a noble height, and lording it over the surrounding country. Every change of season, every change of weather, indeed, every hour of the day, produces some change in the magical hues and shapes of these mountains, and they are regarded by all the good wives, far and near, as perfect barometers. When the weather is fair and settled, they are clothed in blue and purple, and print their bold outlines on the clear evening sky, but, sometimes, when the rest of the landscape is cloudless, they will gather a hood of gray vapours about their summits, which, in the last rays of the setting sun, will glow and light up like a crown of glory.

At the foot of these fairy mountains, the voyager may

have descried the light smoke curling up from a village, whose shingle-roofs gleam among the trees, just where the blue tints of the upland melt away into the fresh green of the nearer landscape. It is a little village of great antiquity, having been founded by some of the Dutch colonists, in the early times of the province, just about the beginning of the government of the good Peter Stuyvesant, (may he rest in peace!) and there were some of the houses of the original settlers standing within a few years, built of small yellow bricks brought from Holland, having latticed windows and gable fronts, surmounted with weather-cocks.

In that same village, and in one of these very houses (which, to tell the precise truth, was sadly time-worn and weather-beaten), there lived many years since, while the country was yet a province of Great Britain, a simple good-natured fellow of the name of Rip Van Winkle. He was a descendant of the Van Winkles who figured so gallantly in the chivalrous days of Peter Stuyvesant, and accompanied him to the siege of Fort Christina. He inherited, however, but little of the martial character of his ancestors. I have observed that he was a simple good-natured man; he was, moreover, a kind neighbour, and an obedient hen-pecked husband. Indeed, to the latter circumstance might be owing that meekness of spirit which gained him such universal popularity; for those men are most apt to be obsequious and conciliating abroad, who are under the discipline of shrews at home. Their tempers, doubtless, are rendered pliant and malleable in the fiery furnace of domestic tribulation; and a curtain lecture is worth all the sermons in the world for teaching the virtues of patience and long-suffering. A termagant wife may, therefore, in some respects, be considered a tolerable blessing; and if so, Rip Van Winkle was thrice blessed.

Certain it is, that he was a great favourite among all the good wives of the village, who, as usual, with the amiable sex, took his part in all family squabbles; and never failed, whenever they talked those matters over in their evening gossiping's, to lay all the blame on Dame Van Winkle. The children of the village, too, would shout with joy whenever he approached. He assisted at their sports, made their playthings, taught them to fly kites and shoot marbles, and told them long stories of ghosts, witches, and Indians. Whenever he went dodging about the village, he was surrounded by a troop of them, hanging on his skirts, clambering on his back, and playing a thousand tricks on him with impunity; and not a dog would bark at him throughout the neighbourhood.

The great error in Rip's composition was an insuperable aversion to all kinds of profitable labour. It could not be from the want of assiduity or perseverance; for he would sit on a wet rock, with a rod as long and heavy as a Tartar's lance, and fish all day without a murmur, even though he should not be encouraged by a single nibble. He would carry a fowling-piece on his shoulder for hours together, trudging through woods and swamps, and uphill and down dale, to shoot a few squirrels or wild pigeons. He would never refuse to assist a neighbour even in the roughest toil, and was a foremost man at all country frolics for husking Indian corn, or building stone-fences; the women of the village, too, used to employ him to run their errands, and to do such little odd jobs as their fewer obliging husbands would not do for them. In a word Rip was ready to attend to anybody's business but his own; but as to doing family duty, and keeping his farm in order, he found it impossible.

In fact, he declared it was of no use to work on his farm; it was the most pestilent little piece of ground in the whole country; everything about it went wrong, and would go wrong, in spite of him. His fences were continually falling to pieces; his cow would either go astray, or get among the cabbages; weeds were sure to grow quicker in his fields than anywhere else; the rain always made a point of setting in just as he had some out-door work to do; so that though his patrimonial estate had dwindled away under his management, acre by acre, until there was little more left than a mere patch of Indian corn and potatoes, yet it was the worst conditioned farm in the neighbourhood.

His children, too, were as ragged and wild as if they belonged to nobody. His son Rip, an urchin begotten in his own likeness, promised to inherit the habits, with the old clothes of his father. He was generally seen trooping like a colt at his mother's heels, equipped in a pair of his father's cast-off galligaskins, which he had much ado to hold up with one hand, as a fine lady does her train in bad weather.

Rip Van Winkle, however, was one of those happy mortals, of foolish, well-oiled dispositions, who take the world easy, eat white bread or brown, whichever can be got with least thought or trouble, and would rather starve on a penny than work for a pound. If left to himself, he would have whistled life away in perfect contentment; but his wife kept continually dinning in his ears about his idleness, his carelessness, and the ruin he was bringing on his family. Morning, noon, and night, her tongue was incessantly going, and everything he said or did was sure to produce a torrent of household eloquence. Rip had but one way of replying to all lectures of the kind, and that, by frequent use, had grown into a habit. He shrugged his shoulders, shook his head, cast up his eyes, but said nothing. This, however, always provoked a fresh volley from his wife; so that he was fain to draw off his forces, and take to the outside of the house - the only side which, in truth, belongs to a hen-pecked husband.

Rip's sole domestic adherent was his dog Wolf, who was as much hen-pecked as his master; for Dame Van Winkle regarded them as companions in idleness, and even looked upon Wolf with an evil eye, as the cause of his master's going so often astray. True it is, in all points of spirit befitting an honourable dog, he was as courageous an animal as ever scoured the woods - but what courage can withstand the ever-during and all-besetting terrors of a woman's tongue? The moment Wolf entered the house his crest fell, his tail drooped to the ground, or curled between his legs, he sneaked about with a gallows air, casting many a sidelong glance at Dame Van Winkle, and at the least flourish of a broom-stick or ladle, he would fly to the door with yelping precipitation.

Times grew worse and worse with Rip Van Winkle as years of matrimony rolled on; a tart temper never mellows with age, and a sharp tongue is the only edged tool that grows keener with constant use. For a long while he used to console himself, when driven from home, by frequenting a kind of perpetual club of the sages, philosophers, and other idle personages of the village; which held its sessions on a bench before a small inn, designated by a rubicund portrait of His Majesty George the Third. Here they used to sit in the shade through a long lazy summer's day, talking listlessly over village gossip, or telling endless sleepy stories about nothing. But it would have been worth any statesman's money to have heard the profound discussions that sometimes took place, when by chance an old newspaper fell into their hands from some passing traveller. How solemnly they would listen to the contents, as drawled out by Derrick Van Bummel, the schoolmaster, a dapper learned little man, who was not to be daunted by the most gigantic word in the dictionary; and how sagely they would deliberate upon public events some months after they had taken place.

The opinions of this junto were completely controlled by Nicholas Veeder, a patriarch of the village, and landlord of the inn, at the door of which he took his seat from morning till night, just moving sufficiently to avoid the sun and keep in the shade of a large tree; so that the neighbours could tell the hour by his movements as accurately as by a sundial. It is true he was rarely heard to speak, but smoked his pipe incessantly. His adherents, however (for every great man has his adherents), perfectly understood him, and knew how to gather his opinions. When anything that was read or related displeased him, he was observed to smoke his pipe vehemently, and to send forth short, frequent and angry puffs; but when pleased, he would inhale the smoke slowly and tranquilly, and emit it in light and placid clouds; and sometimes, taking the pipe from his mouth, and letting the fragrant vapor curl about his nose, would gravely nod his head in token of perfect approbation.

From even this stronghold the unlucky Rip was at length routed by his termagant wife, who would suddenly break in upon the tranquillity of the assemblage and call the members all to naught; nor was that august personage, Nicholas Veeder himself, sacred from the daring tongue of this terrible virago, who charged him outright with encouraging her husband in habits of idleness.

Poor Rip was at last reduced almost to despair; and his only alternative, to escape from the labour of the farm and clamour of his wife, was to take gun in hand and stroll away into the woods. Here he would sometimes seat himself at the foot of a tree, and share the contents of his wallet with Wolf, with whom he sympathized as a fellow-sufferer in persecution. "Poor Wolf," he would say, "thy mistress leads thee a dog's life of it; but never mind, my lad, whilst I live, thou shalt never want a friend to stand by thee!" Wolf would wag his tail, look wistfully in his master's face, and if dogs can feel pity, I verily believe he reciprocated the sentiment with all his heart.

In a long ramble of the kind on a fine autumnal day, Rip had unconsciously scrambled to one of the highest parts of the Catskill mountains. He was after his favourite sport of squirrel shooting, and the still solitudes had echoed and re-echoed with the reports of his gun. Panting and fatigued, he threw himself, late in the afternoon, on a green knoll, covered with mountain herbage, that crowned the brow of a precipice. From an opening between the trees, he could overlook all the lower country for many a mile of rich woodland. He saw at a distance the lordly Hudson, far, far below him, moving on its silent but majestic course, with the reflection of a purple cloud, or the sail of a lagging bark, here and there sleeping on its glassy bosom, and at last losing itself in the blue highlands.

On the other side he looked down into a deep mountain glen, wild, lonely, and shagged, the bottom filled with fragments from the impending cliffs, and scarcely lighted by the reflected rays of the setting sun. For some time, Rip lay musing on this scene; evening was gradually advancing; the mountains began to throw their long blue shadows over the valleys; he saw that it would be dark long before he could reach the village, and he heaved a heavy sigh when he thought of encountering the terrors of Dame Van Winkle.

As he was about to descend, he heard a voice from a distance, hallooing, "Rip Van Winkle! Rip Van Winkle!" He looked round, but could see nothing but a crow winging its solitary flight across the mountain. He thought his fancy must have deceived him, and turned again to descend, when he heard the same cry ring through the still evening air: "Rip Van Winkle! Rip Van Winkle!" - at the same time Wolf bristled up his back, and giving a low growl, skulked to his master's side, looking fearfully down into the glen. Rip now felt a vague apprehension stealing over him; he looked anxiously in the same direction, and perceived a strange figure slowly toiling up the rocks, and bending under the weight of something he carried on his back. He was surprised to see any human being in this lonely and unfrequented place, but supposing it to be some one of the neighbourhoods in need of his assistance, he hastened down to yield it.

On nearer approach he was still more surprised at the singularity of the stranger's appearance. He was a short square-built old fellow, with thick bushy hair, and a grizzled beard. His dress was of the antique Dutch fashion - a cloth jerkin strapped round the waist - several pair of breeches, the outer one of ample volume, decorated with rows of buttons down the sides, and bunches at the knees. He bore on his shoulder a stout keg, that seemed full of liquor, and made signs for Rip to approach and assist him with the load. Though rather shy and distrustful of this new acquaintance, Rip complied with his usual alacrity; and mutually relieving one another, they clambered up a narrow gully, apparently the dry bed of a mountain torrent. As they ascended, rip every now and then heard long rolling peals, like distant thunder, that seemed to issue out of a deep ravine, or rather cleft, between lofty rocks, toward which their rugged path conducted. He paused for an instant, but supposing it to be the muttering of one of those transient thunder-showers which often take place in mountain heights, he proceeded. Passing through the ravine, they came to a hollow, like a small amphitheatre, surrounded by perpendicular precipices, over the brinks of which impending trees shot their branches, so that you only caught glimpses of the azure sky and the bright evening cloud. During the whole time Rip and his companion had laboured on in silence; for though the former marvelled greatly what could be the object of carrying a keg of liquor up this wild mountain, yet there was something strange and incomprehensible about the unknown, that inspired awe and checked familiarity.

On entering the amphitheatre, new objects of wonder presented themselves. On a level spot in the centre was a company of odd-looking personages playing at nine-pins. They were dressed in a quaint outlandish fashion; some wore short doublets, others jerkins, with long knives in their belts, and most of them had enormous breeches, of similar style with that of the guide's. Their visages, too, were peculiar: one had a large beard, broad face, and small piggish eyes: the face of another seemed to consist entirely of nose, and was surmounted by a white sugar-loaf hat set off with a little red cock's tail. They all had beards, of various shapes and colours. There was one who seemed to be the commander. He was a stout old gentleman, with a weather-beaten countenance; he wore a laced doublet, broad belt and hanger, high-crowned hat and feather, red stockings, and high-heeled shoes, with roses in them. The whole group reminded Rip of the figures in an old Flemish painting, in the parlour of Dominie Van Shack, the village parson, and which had been brought over from Holland at the time of the settlement.

What seemed particularly odd to Rip was, that though these folks were evidently amusing themselves, yet they maintained the gravest faces, the most mysterious silence, and were, withal, the melancholiest party of pleasure he had ever witnessed. Nothing interrupted the stillness of the scene but the noise of the balls, which, whenever they were rolled, echoed along the mountains like rumbling peals of thunder.

As Rip and his companion approached them, they suddenly desisted from their play, and stared at him with such fixed statue-like gaze, and such strange, uncouth, lack-lustre countenances, that his heart turned within him, and his knees smote together. His companion now emptied the contents of the keg into large flagons, and made signs to him to wait upon the company. He obeyed with fear and trembling; they quaffed the liquor in profound silence, and then returned to their game.

By degrees Rip's awe and apprehension subsided. He even ventured, when no eye was fixed upon him, to taste the beverage, which he found had much of the flavour of excellent Hollands. He was naturally a thirsty soul, and was soon tempted to repeat the draught. One taste provoked another; and he reiterated his visits to the flagon so often that at length his senses were overpowered, his eyes swam in his head, his head gradually declined, and he fell into a deep sleep.

On waking, he found himself on the green knoll whence he had first seen the old man of the glen. He rubbed his eyes - it was a bright sunny morning. The birds were hopping and twittering among the bushes, and the eagle was wheeling aloft, and breasting the pure mountain breeze. "Surely," thought Rip, "I have not slept here all night." He recalled the occurrences before he fell asleep. The strange man with a keg of liquor - the mountain ravine - the wild retreat among the rocks - the woe-begone party at ninepins - the flagon - "Oh! that flagon! that wicked flagon!" thought Rip - "what excuse shall I make to Dame Van Winkle!"

He looked round for his gun, but in place of the clean well-oiled fowling-piece, he found an old firelock lying by him, the barrel incrusted with rust, the lock falling off, and the stock worm-eaten. He now suspected that the grave restorers of the mountain had put a trick upon him, and having dosed him with liquor, had robbed him of his gun. Wolf, too, had disappeared, but he might have strayed away after a squirrel or partridge. He whistled after him and shouted his name, but all in vain; the echoes repeated his whistle and shout, but no dog was to be seen.

He determined to revisit the scene of the last evening's gambol, and if he met with any of the party, to demand his dog and gun. As he rose to walk, he found himself stiff in the joints, and wanting in his usual activity. "These mountain beds do not agree with me," thought Rip; "and if this frolic should lay me up with a fit of the rheumatism, I shall have a blessed time with Dame Van Winkle." With some difficulty he got down into the glen: he found the gully up which he and his companion had ascended the preceding evening; but to his astonishment a mountain stream was now foaming down it, leaping from rock to rock, and filling the glen with babbling murmurs. He, however, made shift to scramble up its sides, working his toilsome way through thickets of birch, sassafras, and witch-hazel, and sometimes tripped up or entangled by the wild grapevines that twisted their coils or tendrils from tree to tree, and spread a kind of network in his path.

At length he reached to where the ravine had opened

through the cliffs to the amphitheatre; but no traces of such opening remained. The rocks presented a high impenetrable wall over which the torrent came tumbling in a sheet of feathery foam, and fell into a broad deep basin, black from the shadows of the surrounding forest. Here, then, poor Rip was brought to a stand. He again called and whistled after his dog; he was only answered by the cawing of a flock of idle crows, sporting high in air about a dry tree that overhung a sunny precipice; and who, secure in their elevation, seemed to look down and scoff at the poor man's perplexities. What was to be done? the morning was passing away, and Rip felt famished for want of his breakfast. He grieved to give up his dog and gun; he dreaded to meet his wife; but it would not do to starve among the mountains. He shook his head, shouldered the rusty firelock, and, with a heart full of trouble and anxiety, turned his steps homeward.

As he approached the village he met a number of people, but none whom he knew, which somewhat surprised him, for he had thought himself acquainted with everyone in the country round. Their dress, too, was of a different fashion from that to which he was accustomed. They all stared at him with equal marks of surprise, and whenever they cast their eyes upon him, invariably stroked their chins. The constant recurrence of this gesture induced Rip, involuntarily, to do the same, when to his astonishment, he found his beard had grown a foot long!

He had now entered the skirts of the village. A troop of strange children ran at his heels, hooting after him, and pointing at his gray beard. The dogs, too, not one of which he recognized for an old acquaintance, barked at him as he passed. The very village was altered; it was larger and more populous. There were rows of houses which he had never seen before, and those which had been his familiar haunts had disappeared. Strange names were over the doors - strange faces at the windows - everything was strange. His mind now misgave him; he began to doubt whether both he and the world around him were not bewitched. Surely this was his native village, which he had left but the day before. There stood the Catskill mountains - there ran the silver Hudson at a distance - there was every hill and dale precisely as it had always been - Rip was sorely perplexed - "That flagon last night," thought he, "has addled my poor head sadly!"

It was with some difficulty that he found the way to his own house, which he approached with silent awe, expecting every moment to hear the shrill voice of Dame Van Winkle. He found the house gone to decay - the roof fallen in, the windows shattered, and the doors off the hinges. A half-starved dog that looked like Wolf was skulking about it. Rip called him by name, but the cur snarled, showed his teeth, and passed on. This was an unkind cut indeed - "My very dog," sighed poor Rip, "has forgotten me!"

He entered the house, which, to tell the truth, Dame Van Winkle had always kept in neat order. It was empty, forlorn, and apparently abandoned. This desolateness overcame all his connubial fears - he called loudly for his wife and children - the lonely chambers rang for a moment with his voice, and then all again was silence.

He now hurried forth, and hastened to his old resort, the village inn - but it too was gone. A large rickety wooden building stood in its place, with great gaping windows, some of them broken and mended with old hats and petticoats, and over the door was painted, "the Union Hotel, by Jonathan Doolittle." Instead of the great tree that used to shelter the quiet little Dutch inn of yore, there now was reared a tall naked pole, with something on the top that looked like a red night-cap, and from it was fluttering a flag, on which was a singular assemblage of stars and stripes - all this was strange and incomprehensible. He recognized on the sign, however, the ruby face of King George, under which he had smoked so many a peaceful pipe; but even this was singularly metamorphosed. The red coat was changed for one of blue and buff, a sword was held in the hand instead of a sceptre, the head was decorated with a cocked hat, and underneath was painted in large characters, GENERAL WASHINGTON.

There was, as usual, a crowd of folk about the door, but none that Rip recollected. The very character of the people seemed changed. There was a busy, bustling, disputatious tone about it, instead of the accustomed phlegm and drowsy tranquillity. He looked in vain for the sage Nicholas Veeder, with his broad face, double chin, and fair long pipe, uttering clouds of tobacco-smoke instead of idle speeches; or Van Bummel, the schoolmaster, doling forth the contents of an ancient newspaper. In place of these, a lean, bilious-looking fellow, with his pockets full of handbills, was haranguing vehemently about rights of citizens - elections - members of congress - liberty - Bunker's Hill - heroes of seventy-six - and other words, which were a perfect Babylonish jargon to the bewildered Van Winkle.

The appearance of Rip, with his long-grizzled beard, his rusty fowling-piece, his uncouth dress, and an army of women and children at his heels, soon attracted the attention of the tavern politicians. They crowded round him, eyeing him from head to foot with great curiosity. The orator bustled up to him, and, drawing him partly aside, inquired "on which side he voted?" Rip stared in vacant stupidity. Another short but busy little fellow pulled him by the arm, and, rising on tiptoe, inquired in his ear, "Whether he was Federal or Democrat?" Rip was equally at a loss to comprehend the question; when a knowing, self-important old gentleman, in a sharp cocked hat, made his way through the crowd, putting them to the right and left with his elbows as he passed, and planting himself before Van Winkle, with one arm akimbo, the other resting on his cane, his keen eyes and sharp hat penetrating, as it were, into his very soul, demanded in an austere tone, "what brought him to the election with a gun on his shoulder, and a mob at his heels, and whether he meant to breed a riot in the village?" - "Alas! gentlemen," cried Rip, somewhat dismayed, "I am a poor quiet man, a native of the place, and a loyal subject of the king, God bless him!"

Here a general shout burst from the by-standers - "A tory! a tory! a spy! a refugee! hustle him! away with him!" It was with great difficulty that the self-important man in the cocked hat restored order; and, having assumed a tenfold austerity of brow, demanded again of the unknown culprit, what he came there for, and whom he was seeking? The poor man humbly assured him that he meant no harm, but merely came there in search of some of his neighbours, who used to keep about the tavern.

"Well - who are they? - name them."

Rip bethought himself a moment, and inquired, "Where's Nicholas Veeder?"

There was a silence for a little while, when an old man replied, in a thin piping voice, "Nicholas Veeder! why, he is dead and gone these eighteen years! There was a wooden tombstone in the church-yard that used to tell everything about him, but that's rotten and gone too."

"Where's Brom Dutcher?"

"Oh, he went off to the army in the beginning of the war; some say he was killed at the storming of Stony Point - others say he was drowned in a squall at the foot of Antony's Nose. I don't know - he never came back again."

"Where's Van Bummel, the schoolmaster?"

"He went off to the wars too, was a great militia general, and is now in congress."

Rip's heart died away at hearing of these sad changes in his home and friends, and finding himself thus alone in the world.

Every answer puzzled him too, by treating of such enormous lapses of time, and of matters which he could not understand: war - congress - Stony Point; - he had no courage to ask after any more friends, but cried out in despair, "Does nobody here know Rip Van Winkle?"

"Oh, Rip Van Winkle!" exclaimed two or three, "Oh, to be sure! that's Rip van Winkle yonder, leaning against the tree."

Rip looked, and beheld a precise counterpart of himself, as he went up the mountain: apparently as lazy, and certainly as ragged. The poor fellow was now completely confounded. He doubted his own identity, and whether he was himself or another man. In the midst of his bewilderment, the man in the cocked hat demanded who he was, and what was his name?

"God knows," exclaimed he, at his wit's end; "I'm not myself - I'm somebody else - that's me yonder - no - that's somebody else got into my shoes - I was myself last night, but I fell asleep on the mountain, and they've changed my gun, and every thing's changed, and I'm changed, and I can't tell what's my name, or who I am!"

The by-standers began now to look at each other, nod, wink significantly, and tap their fingers against their foreheads. There was a whisper also, about securing the gun, and keeping the old fellow from doing mischief, at the very suggestion of which the self-important man in the cocked hat retired with some precipitation. At this critical moment a fresh comely woman pressed through the throng to get a peep at the Gray-bearded man. She had a chubby child in her arms, which, frightened at his looks, began to cry. "Hush, Rip," cried she, "hush, you little fool; the old man won't hurt you." The name of the child, the air of the mother, the tone of her voice, all awakened a train of recollections in his mind. "What is your name, my good woman?" asked he.

"Judith Gardener."

"And your father's name?"

Rip Van Winkle and other writings

"Ah, poor man, Rip Van Winkle was his name, but it's twenty years since he went away from home with his gun, and never has been heard of since - his dog came home without him; but whether he shot himself, or was carried away by the Indians, nobody can tell. I was then but a little girl."

Rip had but one question more to ask; but he put it with a faltering voice:

"Where's your mother?"

"Oh, she too had died but a short time since; she broke a blood-vessel in a fit of passion at a New-England peddler."

There was a drop of comfort, at least, in this intelligence. The honest man could contain himself no longer. He caught his daughter and her child in his arms. "I am your father!" cried he - "Young Rip Van Winkle once - old Rip Van Winkle now! - Does nobody know poor Rip Van Winkle?"

All stood amazed, until an old woman, tottering out from among the crowd, put her hand to her brow, and peering under it in his face for a moment, exclaimed, "Sure enough! it is Rip van Winkle - it is himself! Welcome home again, old neighbour - Why, where have you been these twenty long years?"

Rip's story was soon told, for the whole twenty years had been to him but as one night. The neighbours stared when they heard it; some were seen to wink at each other, and put their tongues in their cheeks: and the self-important man in the cocked hat, who, when the alarm was over, had returned to the field, screwed down the corners of his mouth, and shook his head - upon which there was a general shaking of the head throughout the assemblage.

It was determined, however, to take the opinion of old Peter Vandebroek, who was seen slowly advancing up the road. He was a descendant of the historian of that name, who wrote one of the earliest accounts of the province. Peter was the most ancient inhabitant of the village, and well versed in all the wonderful events and traditions of the neighbourhood. He recollected Rip at once, and corroborated his story in the most satisfactory manner. He assured the company that it was a fact, handed down from his ancestor the historian, that the Catskill mountains had always been haunted by strange beings. That it was affirmed that the great Hendrick Hudson, the first discoverer of the river and country, kept a kind of vigil there every twenty years, with his crew of the Half-moon; being permitted in this way to revisit the scenes of his enterprise, and keep a guardian eye upon the river, and the great city called by his name. That his father had once seen them in their old Dutch dresses playing at nine-pins in a hollow of the mountain; and that he himself had heard, one summer afternoon, the sound of their balls, like distant peals of thunder.

To make a long story short, the company broke up, and returned to the more important concerns of the election. Rip's daughter took him home to live with her; she had a snug, well-furnished house, and a stout cheery farmer for a husband, whom Rip recollected for one of the urchins that used to climb upon his back. As to Rip's son and heir, who was the ditto of himself, seen leaning against the tree, he was employed to work on the farm; but evinced a hereditary disposition to attend to anything else but his business.

Rip now resumed his old walks and habits; he soon found many of his former cronies, though all rather the worse for the wear and tear of time; and preferred making friends among the rising generation, with whom he soon grew into great favour.

Having nothing to do at home, and being arrived at that happy age when a man can be idle with impunity, he took his place once more on the bench at the inn door, and was reverenced as one of the patriarchs of the village, and a chronicle of the old times "before the war." It was some time before he could get into the regular track of gossip, or could be

Rip Van Winkle and other writings

made to comprehend the strange events that had taken place during his torpor. How that there had been a revolutionary war - that the country had thrown off the yoke of old England - and that, instead of being a subject of his Majesty George the Third, he was now a free citizen of the United States. Rip, in fact, was no politician; the changes of states and empires made but little impression on him; but there was one species of despotism under which he had long groaned, and that was - petticoat government. Happily, that was at an end; he had got his neck out of the yoke of matrimony, and could go in and out whenever he pleased, without dreading the tyranny of Dame Van Winkle. Whenever her name was mentioned, however, he shook his head, shrugged his shoulders, and cast up his eyes; which might pass either for an expression of resignation to his fate, or joy at his deliverance.

He used to tell his story to every stranger that arrived at Mr. Doolittle's hotel. He was observed, at first, to vary on some points every time he told it, which was, doubtless, owing to his having so recently awaked. It at last settled down precisely to the tale I have related, and not a man, woman, or child in the neighbourhood, but knew it by heart. Some always pretended to doubt the reality of it, and insisted that Rip had been out of his head, and that this was one point on which he always remained flighty. The old Dutch inhabitants, however, almost universally gave it full credit. Even to this day they never hear a thunderstorm of a summer afternoon about the Catskill, but they say Hendrick Hudson and his crew are at their game of nine-pins; and it is a common wish of all hen-pecked husbands in the neighbourhood, when life hangs heavy on their hands, that they might have a quieting draught out of Rip Van Winkle's flagon.

NOTE - The foregoing Tale, one would suspect, had been suggested to Mr. Knickerbocker by a little German superstition about the Emperor Frederick der Rothbart, and the Kyphosis Mountain: the subjoined note, however, which he had appended to the tale, shows that it is an absolute fact, narrated with his usual fidelity:

"The story of Rip Van Winkle may seem incredible to many, but nevertheless I give it my full belief, for I know the vicinity of our old Dutch settlements to have been very subject to marvellous events and appearances. Indeed, I have heard many stranger stories than this, in the villages along the Hudson; all of which were too well authenticated to admit of a doubt. I have even talked with Rip Van Winkle myself who, when last I saw him, was a very venerable old man, and so perfectly rational and consistent on every other point, that I think no conscientious person could refuse to take this into the bargain; nay, I have seen a certificate on the subject taken before a country justice and signed with a cross, in the justice's own handwriting. The story, therefore, is beyond the possibility of doubt. D. K."

Postscript

The following are travelling notes from a memorandum-book of Mr. Knickerbocker:

The Keansburg, or Catskill mountains, have always been a region full of fable. The Indians considered them the abode of spirits, who influenced the weather, spreading sunshine or clouds over the landscape, and sending good or bad hunting seasons. They were ruled by an old squaw spirit, said to be their mother. She dwelt on the highest peak of the Catskills, and had charge of the doors of day and night to open and shut them at the proper hour. She hung up the new moons in the skies, and cut up the old ones into stars. In times of drought, if properly propitiated, she would spin light summer clouds out of cobwebs and morning dew, and send them off from the crest of the mountain, flake after flake, like flakes of carded cotton, to float in the air; until, dissolved by the heat of the sun, they would fall in gentle showers, causing the grass to spring, the fruits to ripen, and the corn to grow an inch an hour. If displeased, however, she would brew up clouds black as ink, sitting in the midst of them like a bottle-bellied spider in the midst of its web; and when these clouds broke, woe betide the valleys!

In old times, say the Indian traditions, there was a kind of Manitou or Spirit, who kept about the wildest recesses of the Catskill Mountains, and took a mischievous pleasure in wreaking all kinds of evils and vexations upon the red men. Sometimes he would assume the form of a bear, a panther, or a deer, lead the bewildered hunter a weary chase through tangled forests and among ragged rocks; and then spring off with a loud Ho! Ho! leaving him aghast on the brink of a beetling precipice or raging torrent.

The favourite abode of this Manitou is still shown. It is a great rock or cliff on the loneliest part of the mountains, and, from the flowering vines which clamber about it, and the wild flowers which abound in its neighbourhood, is known by the name of the Garden Rock. Near the foot of it is a small lake, the haunt of the solitary bittern, with water-snakes basking in the sun on the leaves of the pond-lilies which lie on the surface. This place was held in great awe by the Indians, insomuch that the boldest hunter would not pursue his game within its precincts. Once upon a time, however, a hunter who had lost his way, penetrated to the garden rock, where he beheld a number of gourds placed in the crotches of trees. One of these he seized and made off with it, but in the hurry of his retreat he let it fall among the rocks, when a great stream gushed forth, which washed him away and swept him down precipices, where he was dashed to pieces, and the stream made its way to the Hudson, and continues to flow to the present day; being the identical stream known by the name of the Kaaters-kill.

A Legend of Communipaw

TO THE EDITOR OF THE KNICKERBOCKER MAGAZINE.

Sir,

I observed in your last month's periodical, a communication from a Mr. VANDERDONK, giving some information concerning Communipaw. I herewith send you, Mr. Editor, a legend connected with that place; and am much surprised it should have escaped the researches of your very authentic correspondent, as it relates to an edifice scarcely less fated than the House of the Four Chimneys. I give you the legend in its crude and simple state, as I heard it related; it is capable, however, of being dilated, inflated, and dressed up into very imposing shape and dimensions. Should any of your ingenious contributors in this line feel inclined to take it in hand, they will find ample materials, collateral and illustrative, among the papers of the late Rainier Skaats, many years since crier of the court, and keeper of the City Hall, in the city of the Manhattoes; or in the library of that important and utterly renowned functionary, Mr. Jacob Hays, long time high constable, who, in the course of his extensive researches, has amassed an amount of valuable facts, to be rivalled only by that great historical collection, "The Newgate Calendar."

Your humble servant,

BARENT VAN SCHAICK.

THE END.

* * * * * * * * * * * *

GUESTS FROM GIBBET ISLAND

Whoever has visited the ancient and renowned village of Communipaw, may have noticed an old stone building, of most ruinous and sinister appearance. The doors and window-shutters are ready to drop from their hinges; old clothes are stuffed in the broken panes of glass, while legions of half-starved dogs prowl about the premises, and rush out and bark at every passer-by; for your beggarly house in a village is most apt to swarm with profligate and ill-conditioned dogs. What adds to the sinister appearance of this mansion, is a tall frame in front, not little resembling gallows, and which looks as if waiting to accommodate some of the inhabitants with a well-merited airing. It is not gallows, however, but an ancient sign-post; for this dwelling, in the golden days of Communipaw, was one of the most orderly and peaceful of village taverns, where all the public affairs of Communipaw were talked and smoked over. In fact, it was in this very building that Oloffe the Dreamer, and his companions, concerted that great voyage of discovery and colonization, in which they explored Buttermilk Channel, were nearly shipwrecked in the strait of Hell-gate, and finally landed on the Island of Manhattan, and founded the great city of New-Amsterdam.

Even after the province had been cruelly wrested from the sway of their High Mightiness's, by the combined forces of the British and Yankees, this tavern continued its ancient loyalty. It is true, the head of the Prince of Orange disappeared from the sign; a strange bird being painted over it, with the explanatory legend of "DIE WILDE GANS," or The Wild Goose; but this all the world knew to be a sly riddle of the landlord, the worthy Teunis Van Gieson, a knowing man in a small way, who laid his finger beside his nose and winked, when any one studied the signification of his sign, and observed that his goose was hatching, but would join the flock whenever they flew over the water; an enigma which was the perpetual recreation and delight of the loyal but fat-headed burghers of Communipaw.

Under the sway of this patriotic, though discreet and quiet publican, the tavern continued to flourish in primeval tranquillity, and was the resort of all true-hearted Netherlanders, from all parts of Pavonia; who met here quietly and secretly, to smoke and drink the downfall of Briton and Yankee, and success to Admiral Van Tromp.

The only drawback on the comfort of the establishment, was a nephew of mine host, a sister's son, Yan Yost Vander scamp by name, and a real scamp by nature. This unlucky whipster showed an early propensity to mischief, which he gratified in a small way, by playing tricks upon the frequenters of the Wild Goose; putting gunpowder in their pipes, or squibs in their pockets, and astonishing them with an explosion, while they sat nodding round the fire-place in the bar-room; and if perchance a worthy burgher from some distant part of Pavonia had lingered until dark over his potation, it was odds but that young Vander scamp would slip a briar under his horse's tail, as he mounted, and send him clattering along the road, in neck-or-nothing style, to his infinite astonishment and discomfiture.

It may be wondered at, that mine host of the Wild Goose did not turn such a graceless varlet out of doors; but Teunis Van Gieson was an easy-tempered man, and, having no child of his own, looked upon his nephew with almost parental indulgence. His patience and good-nature were doomed to be tried by another inmate of his mansion. This was a cross-grained curmudgeon of a negro, named Pluto, who was a kind of enigma in Communipaw. Where he came from, nobody knew. He was found one morning, after a storm, cast like a sea-monster on the strand, in front of the Wild Goose, and lay

Rip Van Winkle and other writings

there, more dead than alive. The neighbours gathered round, and speculated on this production of the deep; whether it was fish or flesh, or a compound of both, commonly yclept a merman. The kind-hearted Tenuis Van Gieson, seeing that he wore the human form, took him into his house, and warmed him into life. By degrees, he showed signs of intelligence, and even uttered sounds very much like language, but which no one in Communipaw could understand. Some thought him a negro just from Guinea, who had either fallen overboard, or escaped from a slave-ship. Nothing, however, could ever draw from him any account of his origin. When questioned on the subject, he merely pointed to Gibbet-Island, a small rocky islet, which lies in the open bay, just opposite to Communipaw, as if that were his native place, though everybody knew it had never been inhabited.

In the process of time, he acquired something of the Dutch language, that is to say, he learnt all its vocabulary of oaths and maledictions, with just words sufficient to string them together. "Donder en blicksen!" (Thunder and lightning,) was the gentlest of his ejaculations. For years he kept about the Wild Goose, more like one of those familiar spirits, or household goblins, that we read of, than like a human being. He acknowledged allegiance to no one, but performed various domestic offices, when it suited his humour; waiting occasionally on the guests; grooming the horses, cutting wood, drawing water; and all this without being ordered. Lay any command on him, and the stubborn sea-urchin was sure to rebel. He was never so much at home, however, as when on the water, plying about in skiff or canoe, entirely alone, fishing, crabbing, or grabbing for oysters, and would bring home quantities for the larder of the Wild Goose, which he would throw down at the kitchen door, with a growl. No wind nor weather deterred him from launching forth on his favourite element: indeed, the wilder the weather, the more he seemed to enjoy it. If a storm was brewing, he was sure to put off from shore; and would be seen far out in the bay, his light skiff dancing like a feather on the waves, when sea and sky were all in a turmoil, and the stoutest ships were fain to lower their sails. Sometimes, on such occasions, he would be absent for days together. How he weathered the tempest, and how and where he subsisted, no one could divine, nor did any one venture to ask, for all had an almost superstitious awe of him. Some of the Communipaw oystermen declared that they had more than once seen him suddenly disappear, canoe and all, as if they plunged beneath the waves, and after a while come up again, in quite a different part of the bay; whence they concluded that he could live under water like that notable species of wild duck, commonly called the Hell-diver. All began to consider him in the light of a foul-weather bird, like the Mother Carey's Chicken, or Stormy Petrel; and whenever they saw him putting far out in his skiff, in cloudy weather, made up their minds for a storm.

The only being for whom he seemed to have any liking, was Yan Yost Vander scamp, and him he liked for his very wickedness. He in a manner took the boy under his tutelage, prompted him to all kinds of mischief, aided him in every wild, harum-scarum freak, until the lad became the complete scapegrace of the village; a pest to his uncle, and to everyone else. Nor were his pranks confined to the land; he soon learned to accompany old Pluto on the water. Together these worthies would cruise about the broad bay, and all the neighbouring straits and rivers; poking around in skiffs and canoes; robbing the set-nets of the fishermen; landing on remote coasts, and laying waste orchards and water-melon patches; in short, carrying on a complete system of piracy, on a small scale, Piloted by Pluto, the youthful Vander scamp soon became acquainted with all the bays, rivers, creeks, and inlets of the watery world around him; could navigate from the Hook to Spiting-devil on the darkest night, and learned to set even the terrors of Hell-gate at defiance.

At length, negro and boy suddenly disappeared, and days

and weeks elapsed, but without tidings of them. Some said they must have run away and gone to sea; others jocosely hinted, that old Pluto, being no other than his namesake in disguise, had spirited away the boy to the nether regions. All, however, agreed in one thing, that the village was well rid of them.

In the process of time, the good Tenuis van Gibson slept with his fathers, and the tavern remained shut up, waiting for a claimant, for the next heir was Yan Yost Vander scamp, and he had not been heard of for years. At length, one day, a boat was seen pulling for the shore, from a long, black, rakish-looking schooner, that lay at anchor in the bay. The boat's crew seemed worthy of the craft from which they debarked. Never had such a set of noisy, roistering, swaggering varlets landed in peaceful Communipaw. They were outlandish in garb and demeanour, and were headed by a rough, burly, bully ruffian, with fiery whiskers, a copper nose, a scar across his face, and a great Flounderish beaver slouched on one side of his head, in whom, to their dismay, the quiet inhabitants were made to recognize their early pest, Yan Yost Vander scamp. The rear of this hopeful gang was brought up by old Pluto, who had lost an eye, grown grizzly-headed, and looked more like a devil than ever. Vander scamp renewed his acquaintance with the old burghers, much against their will, and in a manner not at all to their taste. He slapped them familiarly on the back, gave them an iron grip of the hand, and was hail fellow well met. According to his own account, he had been all the world over; had made money by bags full; had ships in every sea, and now meant to turn the Wild Goose into a country seat, where he and his comrades, all rich merchants from foreign parts, might enjoy themselves in the interval of their voyages. Sure enough, in a little while there was a complete metamorphose of the Wild Goose. From being a quiet, peaceful Dutch public house, it became a most riotous, uproarious private dwelling; a complete rendezvous for boisterous men of the seas, who came here to have what they called a "blow out" on dry land,

and might be seen at all hours, lounging about the door, or lolling out of the windows; swearing among themselves, and cracking rough jokes on every passer-by. The house was fitted up, too, in so strange a manner: hammocks slung to the walls, instead of bedsteads; odd kinds of furniture, of foreign fashion; bamboo couches, Spanish chairs; pistols, cutlasses, and blunderbusses, suspended on every peg; silver crucifixes on the mantel-pieces, silver candle-sticks and porringers on the tables, contrasting oddly with the pewter and Delf ware of the original establishment. And then the strange amusements of these sea-monsters! Pitching Spanish dollars, instead of quoits; firing blunderbusses out of the window; shooting at a mark, or at any unhappy dog, or cat, or pig, or barn-door fowl, that might happen to come within reach.

The only being who seemed to relish their rough wiggery, was old Pluto; and yet he led but a dog's life of it; for they practised all kinds of manual jokes upon him; kicked him about like a foot-ball; shook him by his grizzly mop of wool, and never spoke to him without coupling a curse by way of adjective to his name, and consigning him to the infernal regions. The old fellow, however, seemed to like them the better, the more they cursed him, though his utmost expression of pleasure never amounted to more than the growl of a petted bear, when his ears are rubbed.

Old Pluto was the ministering spirit at the orgies of the Wild Goose; and such orgies as took place there! Such drinking, singing, whooping, swearing; with an occasional interlude of quarrelling and fighting. The noisier grew the revel, the elder Pluto plied the potations, until the guests would become frantic in their merriment, smashing everything to pieces, and throwing the house out of the windows. Sometimes, after a drinking bout, they sallied forth and scoured the village, to the dismay of the worthy burghers, who gathered their women within doors, and would have shut up the house. Vander scamp, however, was not to be rebuffed. He insisted on renewing acquaintance with his old neighbours, and on introducing his friends, the merchants, to their families; swore he was on the look-out for a wife, and meant, before he stopped, to find husbands for all their daughters. So, will-ye, nil-ye, sociable he was; swaggered about their best parlours, with his hat on one side of his head; sat on the good wife's nicely-waxed mahogany table, kicking his heels against the carved and polished legs; kissed and tousled the young vrouws; and, if they frowned and pouted, gave them a gold rosary, or a sparkling cross, to put them in good humour again.

Sometimes nothing would satisfy him, but he must have some of his old neighbours to dinner at the Wild Goose. There was no refusing him, for he had got the complete upper-hand of the community, and the peaceful burghers all stood in awe of him. But what a time would the quiet, worthy men have, among these rake-hells, who would delight to astound them with the most extravagant gunpowder tales, embroidered with all kinds of foreign oaths; clink the can with them; pledge them in deep potations; bawl drinking songs in their ears; and occasionally fire pistols over their heads, or under the table, and then laugh in their faces, and ask them how they liked the smell of gunpowder.

Thus was the little village of Communipaw for a time like the unfortunate wight possessed with devils; until Vander scamp and his brother merchants would sail on another trading voyage, when the Wild Goose would be shut up, and everything relapse into quiet, only to be disturbed by his next visitation.

The mystery of all these proceedings gradually dawned upon the tardy intellects of Communipaw. These were the times of the notorious Captain Kidd, when the American harbours were the resorts of piratical adventurers of all kinds, who, under pretext of mercantile voyages, scoured the West Indies, made plundering descents upon the Spanish Main, visited even the remote Indian Seas, and then came to dispose of their booty, have their revels, and fit out new expeditions, in the English colonies.

Vander scamp had served in this hopeful school, and having risen to importance among the buccaneers, had pitched upon his native village and early home, as a quiet, out-of-the-way, unsuspected place, where he and his comrades, while anchored at New York, might have their feasts, and concert their plans, without molestation.

At length the attention of the British government was called to these piratical enterprises, that were becoming so frequent and outrageous. Vigorous measures were taken to check and punish them. Several of the most noted freebooters were caught and executed, and three of Vander scamp's chosen comrades, the most riotous swash-bucklers of the Wild Goose, were hanged in chains on Gibbet-Island, in full sight of their favourite resort. As to Vander scamp himself, he and his man Pluto again disappeared, and it was hoped by the people of Communipaw that he had fallen in some foreign brawl, or been swung on some foreign gallows.

For a time, therefore, the tranquillity of the village was restored; the worthy Dutchmen once more smoked their pipes in peace, eying, with peculiar complacency, their old pests and terrors, the pirates, dangling and drying in the sun, on Gibbet-Island.

This perfect calm was doomed at length to be ruffled. The fiery persecution of the pirates gradually subsided. Justice was satisfied with the examples that had been made, and there was no more talk of Kidd, and the other heroes of like kidney. On a calm summer evening, a boat, somewhat heavily laden, was seen pulling into Communipaw. What was the surprise and disquiet of the inhabitants, to see Yan Yost Vander scamp seated at the helm, and his man Pluto tugging at the oars! Vander scamp, however, was apparently an altered man. He brought home with him a wife, who seemed to be a shrew, and to have the upper-hand of him. He no longer was the

Rip Van Winkle and other writings

swaggering, bully ruffian, but affected the regular merchant, and talked of retiring from business, and settling down quietly, to pass the rest of his days in his native place.

The Wild Goose mansion was again opened, but with diminished splendour, and no riot. It is true, Vander scamp had frequent nautical visitors, and the sound of revelry was occasionally overheard in his house; but everything seemed to be done under the rose; and old Pluto was the only servant that officiated at these orgies. The visitors, indeed, were by no means of the turbulent stamp of their predecessors; but quiet, mysterious traders, full of nods, and winks, and hieroglyphic signs, with whom, to use their cant phrase, "everything was smug." Their ships came to anchor at night in the lower bay; and, on a private signal, Vander scamp would launch his boat, and accompanied solely by his man Pluto, would make them mysterious visits. Sometimes boats pulled in at night, in front of the Wild Goose, and various articles of merchandise were landed in the dark, and spirited away, nobody knew whither. One of the more curious of the inhabitants kept watch, and caught a glimpse of the features of some of these night visitors, by the casual glance of a lantern, and declared that he recognized more than one of the freebooting frequenters of the Wild Goose, in former times; from whence he concluded that Vander scamp was at his old game, and that this mysterious merchandise was nothing more nor less than piratical plunder. The more charitable opinion, however, was, that Vander scamp and his comrades, having been driven from their old line of business, by the "oppressions of government," had resorted to smuggling to make both ends meet.

Be that as it may: I come now to the extraordinary fact, which is the butt-end of this story. It happened late one night, that Yan Yost Vander scamp was returning across the broad bay, in his light skiff, rowed by his man Pluto. He had been carousing on board of a vessel, newly arrived, and was somewhat obfuscated in intellect, by the liquor he had imbibed. It was a still, sultry night; a heavy mass of lurid clouds was rising in the west, with the low muttering of distant thunder. Vander scamp called on Pluto to pull lustily, that they might get home before the gathering storm. The old negro made no reply, but shaped his course so as to skirt the rocky shores of Gibbet-Island. A faint creaking overhead caused Vander scamp to cast up his eyes, when, to his horror, he beheld the bodies of his three pot companions and brothers in iniquity dangling in the moonlight, their rags fluttering, and their chains creaking, as they were slowly swung backward and forward by the rising breeze.

"What do you mean, you blockhead!" cried Vander scamp, "by pulling so close to the island?"

"I thought you'd be glad to see your old friends once more," growled the negro; "you were never afraid of a living man, what do you fear from the dead?"

"Who's afraid?" hiccupped Vander scamp, partly heated by liquor, partly nettled by the jeer of the negro; "who's afraid! Hang me, but I would be glad to see them once more, alive or dead, at the Wild Goose. Come, my lads in the wind!" continued he, taking a draught, and flourishing the bottle above his head, "here's fair weather to you in the other world; and if you should be walking the rounds to-night, odds fish! but I'll be happy if you will drop in to supper."

A dismal creaking was the only reply. The wind blew loud and shrill, and as it whistled round the gallows, and among the bones, sounded as if there were laughing and gibbering in the air. Old Pluto chuckled to himself, and now pulled for home. The storm burst over the voyagers, while they were yet far from shore. The rain fell in torrents, the thunder crashed and pealed, and the lightning kept up an incessant blaze. It was stark midnight, before they landed at Communipaw.

Dripping and shivering, Vander scamp crawled homeward.

He was completely sobered by the storm; the water soaked from without, having diluted and cooled the liquor within. Arrived at the Wild Goose, he knocked timidly and dubiously at the door, for he dreaded the reception he was to experience from his wife. He had reason to do so. She met him at the threshold, in a precious ill humour.

"Is this a time," said she, "to keep people out of their beds, and to bring home company, to turn the house upside down?"

"Company?" said Vander scamp, meekly; "I have brought no company with me, wife."

"No, indeed! they have got here before you, but by your invitation; and blessed-looking company they are, truly!"

Vander scamp's knees smote together. "For the love of heaven, where are they, wife?"

"Where? --why, in the blue-room, up-stairs, making themselves as much at home as if the house were their own."

Vander scamp made a desperate effort, scrambled up to the room, and threw open the door. Sure enough, there at a table, on which burned a light as blue as brimstone, sat the three guests from Gibbet-Island, with halters round their necks, and bobbing their cups together, as if they were hob-or-knobbing, and trolling the old Dutch freebooter's glee, since translated into English:

"For three merry lads be we, and three merry lads be we; I on the land, and thou on the sand, And Jack on the gallows-tree."

Vander scamp saw and heard no more. Starting back with horror, he missed his footing on the landing-place, and fell from the top of the stairs to the bottom. He was taken up speechless, and, either from the fall or the fright, was buried in the yard of the little Dutch church at Bergen, on the following Sunday.

From that day forward, the fate of the Wild Goose was sealed. It was pronounced a haunted house, and avoided accordingly. No one inhabited it but Vander scamp's shrew of a widow, and old Pluto, and they were considered but little better than its hobgoblin visitors. Pluto grew more and more haggard and morose, and looked more like an imp of darkness than a human being. He spoke to no one, but went about muttering to himself; or, as some hinted, talking with the devil, who, though unseen, was ever at his elbow. Now and then he was seen pulling about the bay alone, in his skiff, in dark weather, or at the approach of night-fall; nobody could tell why, unless on an errand to invite more guests from the gallows. Indeed, it was affirmed that the Wild Goose still continued to be a house of entertainment for such guests, and that on stormy nights, the blue chamber was occasionally illuminated, and sounds of diabolical merriment were overheard, mingling with the howling of the tempest. Some treated these as idle stories, until on one such night, it was about the time of the equinox, there was a horrible uproar in the Wild Goose, that could not be mistaken. It was not so much the sound of revelry, however, as strife, with two or three piercing shrieks, that pervaded every part of the village. Nevertheless, no one thought of hastening to the spot. On the contrary, the honest burghers of Communipaw drew their night-caps over their ears, and buried their heads under the bed-clothes, at the thoughts of Vander scamp and his gallows companions.

The next morning, some of the bolder and more curious undertook to reconnoitre. All was quiet and lifeless at the Wild Goose. The door yawned wide open, and had evidently been open all night, for the storm had beaten into the house. Gathering more courage from the silence and apparent desertion, they gradually ventured over the threshold. The house had indeed the air of having been possessed by devils. Everything was topsy-turvy; trunks had been broken open, and chests of drawers and corner cupboards turned inside out, as in a time of general sack and pillage; but the most woeful sight was the widow of Yan Yost Vander scamp, extended a corpse on the floor of the blue-chamber, with the marks of a deadly gripe on the wind-pipe.

All now was conjecture and dismay at Communipaw; and the disappearance of old Pluto, who was nowhere to be found, gave rise to all kinds of wild surmises. Some suggested that the negro had betrayed the house to some of Vander scamp's buccaneering associates, and that they had decamped together with the booty; others surmised that the negro was nothing more nor less than a devil incarnate, who had now accomplished his ends, and made off with his dues. Events, however, vindicated the negro from this last imputation. His skiff was picked up, drifting about the bay, bottom upward, as if wrecked in a tempest; and his body was found, shortly afterward, by some Communipaw fishermen, stranded among the rocks of Gibbet-Island, near the foot of the pirates' gallows. The fishermen shook their heads, and observed that old Pluto had ventured once too often to invite Guests from Gibbet-Island.

Christmas

A man might then behold
At Christmas, in each hall
Good fires to curb the cold,
And meat for great and small.
The neighbours were friendly bidden,
And all had welcome true,
The poor from the gates were not chidden,
When this old cap was new.

Old Song.

There is nothing in England that exercises a more delightful spell over my imagination than the lingering of the holiday customs and rural games of former times. They recall the pictures my fancy used to draw in the May morning of life, when as yet I only knew the world through books, and believed it to be all those poets had painted it; and they bring with them the flavour of those honest days of yore, in which, perhaps with equal fallacy, I am apt to think the world was more home-bred, social, and joyous than at present. I regret to say that they are daily growing more and more faint, being gradually worn away by time, but still more obliterated by modern fashion. They resemble those picturesque morsels of Gothic architecture which we see crumbling in various parts of the country, partly dilapidated by the waste of ages, and partly lost in the additions and alterations of latter days. Poetry, however, clings with cherishing fondness about the rural game

Rip Van Winkle and other writings

and holiday revel, from which it has derived so many of its themes—as the ivy winds its rich foliage about the Gothic arch and mouldering tower, gratefully repaying their support by clasping together their tottering remains, and, as it were, embalming them in verdure.

Of all the old festivals, however, that of Christmas awakens the strongest and most heartfelt associations. There is a tone of solemn and sacred feeling that blends with our conviviality, and lifts the spirit to a state of hallowed and elevated enjoyment. The services of the church about this season are extremely tender and inspiring. They dwell on the beautiful story of the origin of our faith, and the pastoral scenes that accompanied its announcement. They gradually increase in fervour and pathos during the season of Advent, until they break forth in full jubilee on the morning that brought peace and good-will to men. I do not know a grander effect of music on the moral feelings than to hear the full choir and the pealing organ performing a Christmas anthem in a cathedral, and filling every part of the vast pile with triumphant harmony.

It is a beautiful arrangement, also, derived from days of yore, that this festival, which commemorates the announcement of the religion of peace and love, has been made the season for gathering together of family connections, and drawing closer again those bands of kindred hearts which the cares and pleasures and sorrows of the world are continually operating to cast loose; of calling back the children of a family who have launched forth in life, and wandered widely asunder, once more to assemble about the paternal hearth, that rallying-place of the affections, there to grow young and loving again among the endearing mementoes of childhood.

There is something in the very season of the year that gives a charm to the festivity of Christmas. At other times we derive a great portion of our pleasures from the mere beauties of nature. Our feelings sally forth and dissipate themselves over the sunny landscape, and we "live abroad and everywhere." The song of the bird, the murmur of the stream, the breathing fragrance of spring, the soft voluptuousness of summer, the golden pomp of autumn; earth with its mantle of refreshing green, and heaven with its deep delicious blue and its cloudy magnificence, all fill us with mute but exquisite delight, and we revel in the luxury of mere sensation. But in the depth of winter, when nature lies despoiled of every charm, and wrapped in her shroud of sheeted snow, we turn for our gratifications to moral sources. The dreariness and desolation of the landscape, the short gloomy days and darksome nights, while they circumscribe our wanderings, shut in our feelings also from rambling abroad, and make us more keenly disposed for the pleasures of the social circle. Our thoughts are more concentrated; our friendly sympathies more aroused. We feel more sensibly the charm of each other's society, and are brought more closely together by dependence on each other for enjoyment. Heart calleth unto heart; and we draw our pleasures from the deep wells of living kindness, which lie in the quiet recesses of our bosoms; and which, when resorted to, furnish forth the pure element of domestic felicity.

The pitchy gloom without makes the heart dilate on entering the room filled with the glow and warmth of the evening fire. The ruddy blaze diffuses an artificial summer and sunshine through the room, and lights up each countenance into a kindlier welcome. Where does the honest face of hospitality expand into a broader and more cordial smile—where is the shy glance of love more sweetly eloquent—than by the winter fireside? and as the hollow blast of wintry wind rushes through the hall, claps the distant door, whistles about the casement, and rumbles down the chimney, what can be more grateful than that feeling of sober and sheltered security with which we look round upon the comfortable chamber and the scene of domestic hilarity?

The English, from the great prevalence of rural habits throughout every class of society, have always been fond of those festivals and holidays which agreeably interrupt the stillness of country life; and they were, in former days, particularly observant of the religious and social rites of Christmas. It is inspiring to read even the dry details which some antiquarians have given of the quaint humours, the burlesque pageants, the complete abandonment to mirth and good-fellowship, with which this festival was celebrated. It seemed to throw open every door, and unlock every heart. It brought the peasant and the peer together, and blended all ranks in one warm generous flow of joy and kindness. The old halls of castles and manor-houses resounded with the harp and the Christmas carol, and their ample boards groaned under the weight of hospitality. Even the poorest cottage welcomed the festive season with green decorations of bay and holly—the cheerful fire glanced its rays through the lattice, inviting the passenger to raise the latch, and join the gossip knot huddled round the hearth, beguiling the long evening with legendary jokes and oft-told Christmas tales.

One of the least pleasing effects of modern refinement is the havoc it has made among the hearty old holiday customs. It has completely taken off the sharp touching and spirited reliefs of these embellishments of life, and has worn down society into a smoother and more polished, but certainly a less characteristic surface. Many of the games and ceremonials of Christmas have entirely disappeared, and, like the sherris sack of old Falstaff, are become matters of speculation and dispute among commentators. They flourished in times full of spirit and lustihood, when men enjoyed life roughly, but heartily and vigorously; times wild and picturesque, which have furnished poetry with its richest materials, and the drama with its most attractive variety of characters and manners. The world has become more worldly. There is more of dissipation, and less of enjoyment. Pleasure has expanded into a broader, but a shallower stream, and has forsaken many of those deep and quiet channels where it flowed sweetly through the calm bosom of domestic life. Society has acquired a more enlightened and elegant tone; but it has lost many of its strong local peculiarities, its home-bred feelings, its honest fireside delights. The traditionary customs of golden-hearted antiquity, its feudal hospitalities, and lordly wassailing's, have passed away with the baronial castles and stately manor-houses in which they were celebrated. They comported with the shadowy hall, the great oaken gallery, and the tapestried parlour, but are unfitted to the light showy saloons and gay drawing-rooms of the modern villa.

Shorn, however, as it is, of its ancient and festive honours, Christmas is still a period of delightful excitement in England. It is gratifying to see that home-feeling completely aroused which seems to hold so powerful a place in every English bosom. The preparations making on every side for the social board that is again to unite friends and kindred; the presents of good cheer passing and repassing, those tokens of regard, and quickness of kind feelings; the evergreens distributed about houses and churches, emblems of peace and gladness; all these have the most pleasing effect in producing fond associations, and kindling benevolent sympathies. Even the sound of the waits, rude as may be their minstrelsy, breaks upon the mid-watches of a winter night with the effect of perfect harmony. As I have been awakened by them in that still and solemn hour, "when deep sleep fillet upon man," I have listened with a hushed delight, and connecting them with the sacred and joyous occasion, have almost fancied them into another celestial choir, announcing peace and good-will to mankind.

How delightfully the imagination, when wrought upon by these moral influences, turns everything to melody and beauty: The very crowing of the cock, who is sometimes heard in the profound repose of the country, "telling the night watches to his feathery dames," was thought by the common people to announce the approach of this sacred festival: —

> *"Some say that ever 'gains that season comes*
>
> *Wherein our Saviour's birth is celebrated,*
>
> *This bird of dawning signet all night long:*
>
> *And then, they say, no spirit dares stir abroad;*
>
> *The nights are wholesome—then no planets strike,*
>
> *No fairy tales, no witch hath power to charm,*
>
> *So hallowed and so gracious is the time."*

Amidst the general call to happiness, the bustle of the spirits, and stir of the affections, which prevail at this period, what bosom can remain insensible? It is, indeed, the season of regenerated feeling—the season for kindling, not merely the fire of hospitality in the hall, but the genial flame of charity in the heart.

The scene of early love again rises green to memory beyond the sterile waste of years; and the idea of home, fraught with the fragrance of home-dwelling joys, re-animates the drooping spirit, —as the Arabian breeze will sometimes waft the freshness of the distant fields to the weary pilgrim of the desert. Stranger and sojourner as I are in the land—though for me no social hearth may blaze, no hospitable roof throw open its doors, nor the warm grasp of friendship welcome me at the threshold—yet I feel the influence of the season beaming into my soul from the happy looks of those around me. Surely happiness is reflective, like the light of heaven; and every countenance, bright with smiles, and glowing with innocent enjoyment, is a mirror transmitting to others the rays of a supreme and ever-shining benevolence. He who can turn churlishly away from contemplating the felicity of his fellow-beings, and sit down darkling and repining in his loneliness when all around is joyful, may have his moments of strong excitement and selfish gratification, but he wants the genial and social sympathies which constitute the charm of a merry Christmas.

Communipaw

Sir,

I observe, with pleasure, that you are performing from time to time a pious duty, imposed upon you, I may say, by the name you have adopted as your titular standard, in following in the footsteps of the venerable KNICKERBOCKER, and gleaning every fact concerning the early times of the Manhaters which may have escaped his hand. I trust, therefore, a few particulars, legendary and statistical, concerning a place which figures conspicuously in the early pages of his history, will not be unacceptable. I allude, Sir, to the ancient and renowned village of Communipaw, which, according to the veracious Diedrich, and to equally veracious tradition, was the first spot where our ever-to-be-lamented Dutch progenitors planted their standard and cast the seeds of empire, and from whence subsequently sailed the memorable expedition under Oloffe the Dreamer, which landed on the opposite island of Manhattan, and founded the present city of New-York, the city of dreams and speculations.

Communipaw, therefore, may truly be called the parent of New-York; yet it is an astonishing fact, that though immediately opposite to the great city it has produced, from whence its red roofs and tin weather-cocks can actually be descried peering above the surrounding apple orchards, it should be almost as rarely visited, and as little known by the inhabitants of the metropolis, as if it had been locked up among the Rocky Mountains. Sir, I think there is something unnatural in this, especially in these times of ramble and research, when our citizens are antiquity-hunting in every part of the world. Curiosity, like charity, should begin at home; and I would enjoin it on our worthy burghers, especially those of the real Knickerbocker breed, before they send their sons abroad to wonder and grow wise among the remains of Greece and Rome, to let them make a tour of ancient Pavonia, from Wee hawk even to the Kills, and meditate, with filial reverence, on the moss-grown mansions of Communipaw. Sir, I regard this much neglected village as one of the most remarkable places in the country. The intelligent traveller, as he looks down upon it from the Bergen Heights, modestly nestled among its cabbage-gardens, while the great flaunting city it has begotten is stretching far and wide on the opposite side of the bay, the intelligent traveller, I say, will be filled with astonishment; not, Sir, at the village of Communipaw, which in truth is a very small village, but at the almost incredible fact that so small a village should have produced so great a city. It looks to him, indeed, like some squat little dame, with a tall grenadier of a son strutting by her side; or some simple-hearted hen that has unwittingly hatched out a long-legged turkey.

But this is not all for which Communipaw is remarkable. Sir, it is interesting on another account. It is to the ancient province of the New-Netherlands and the classic era of the Dutch dynasty, what Herculaneum and Pompeii are to ancient Rome and the glorious days of the empire. Here everything remains in status quo, as it was in the days of Oloffe the Dreamer, Walter the Doubter, and the other worthies of the golden age; the same broad-brimmed hats and broad-bottomed breeches; the same knee-buckles and shoe-buckles; the same close-quilled caps and linsey-woolsey short-gowns and petticoats; the same implements and utensils and forms and fashions; in a word, Communipaw at the present day is a picture of what New-Amsterdam was before the conquest. The "intelligent traveller" aforesaid, as he treads its streets, is struck with the primitive character of everything around him.

Instead of Grecian temples for dwelling-houses, with a great column of pine boards in the way of every window, he beholds high peaked roofs, gable ends to the street, with weather-cocks at top, and windows of all sorts and sizes; large ones for the grown-up members of the family, and little ones for the little folk. Instead of cold marble porches, with close-locked doors and brass knockers, he sees the doors hospitably open; the worthy burgher smoking his pipe on the old-fashioned stoop in front, with his "vrouw" knitting beside him; and the cat and her kittens at their feet sleeping in the sunshine.

Astonished at the obsolete and "old world" air of everything around him, the intelligent traveller demands how all this has come to pass. Herculaneum and Pompeii remain, it is true, unaffected by the varying fashions of centuries; but they were buried by a volcano and preserved in ashes. What charmed spell has kept this wonderful little place unchanged, though in sight of the most changeful city in the universe? Has it, too, been buried under its cabbage-gardens, and only dug out in modern days for the wonder and edification of the world? The reply involves a point of history, worthy of notice and record, and reflecting immortal honour on Communipaw.

At the time when New-Amsterdam was invaded and conquered by British foes, as has been related in the history of the venerable Diedrich, a great dispersion took place among the Dutch inhabitants. Many, like the illustrious Peter Stuyvesant, buried themselves in rural retreats in the Bowery; others, like Wolfelt Acker, took refuge in various remote parts of the Hudson; but there was one staunch, unconquerable band that determined to keep together, and preserve themselves, like seed corn, for the future fructification and perpetuity of the Knickerbocker race. These were headed by one Garret Van Horne, a gigantic Dutchman, the Pelayo of the New-Netherlands. Under his guidance, they retreated across the bay and buried themselves among the marshes of ancient Pavonia, as did the followers of Pelayo among the mountains

Rip Van Winkle and other writings

of Asturias, when Spain was overrun by its Arabian invaders.

The gallant Van Horne set up his standard at Communipaw, and invited all those to rally under it, who were true Netherlanders at heart, and determined to resist all foreign intermixture or encroachment. A strict non-intercourse was observed with the captured city; not a boat ever crossed to it from Communipaw, and the English language was rigorously tabooed throughout the village and its dependencies. Every man was sworn to wear his hat, cut his coat, build his house, and harness his horses, exactly as his father had done before him; and to permit nothing but the Dutch language to be spoken in his household.

As a citadel of the place, and a strong-hold for the preservation and defence of everything Dutch, the gallant Van Horne erected a lordly mansion, with a chimney perched at every corner, which thence derived the aristocratical name of "The House of the Four Chimneys." Hither he transferred many of the precious reliques of New-Amsterdam; the great round-crowned hat that once covered the capacious head of Walter the Doubter, and the identical shoe with which Peter the Headstrong kicked his pusillanimous councillors downstairs. St. Nicholas, it is said, took this loyal house under his especial protection; and a Dutch soothsayer predicted, that as long as it should stand, Communipaw would be safe from the intrusion either of Briton or Yankee.

In this house would the gallant Van Home and his compeers hold frequent councils of war, as to the possibility of re-conquering the province from the British; and here would they sit for hours, nay, days, together smoking their pipes and keeping watch upon the growing city of New-York; groaning in spirit whenever they saw a new house erected or ship launched, and persuading themselves that Admiral Van Tromp would one day or other arrive to sweep out the invaders with the broom which he carried at his mast-head.

Years rolled by, but Van Tromp never arrived. The British strengthened themselves in the land, and the captured city flourished under their domination. Still, the worthies of Communipaw would not despair; something or other, they were sure, would turn up to restore the power of the Hogen Mogens, the Lord States-General; so, they kept smoking and smoking, and watching and watching, and turning the same few thoughts over and over in a perpetual circle, which is commonly called deliberating. In the meantime, being hemmed up within a narrow compass, between the broad bay and the Bergen hills, they grew poorer and poorer, until they had scarce the wherewithal to maintain their pipes in fuel during their endless deliberations.

And now must I relate a circumstance which will call for a little exertion of faith on the part of the reader; but I can only say that if he doubts it, he had better not utter his doubts in Communipaw, as it is among the religious beliefs of the place. It is, in fact, nothing more nor less than a miracle, worked by the blessed St. Nicholas, for the relief and sustenance of this loyal community.

It so happened, in this time of extremity, that in the course of cleaning the House of the Four Chimneys, by an ignorant housewife who knew nothing of the historic value of the reliques it contained, the old hat of Walter the Doubter and the executive shoe of Peter the Headstrong were thrown out of doors as rubbish. But mark the consequence. The good St. Nicholas kept watch over these precious reliques, and wrought out of them a wonderful providence.

The hat of Walter the Doubter falling on a stercoraceous heap of compost, in the rear of the house, began forthwith to vegetate. Its broad brim, spread forth grandly and exfoliated, and its round crown swelled and crimped and consolidated until the whole became a prodigious cabbage, rivalling in magnitude the capacious head of the Doubter. In a word, it

Rip Van Winkle and other writings

was the origin of that renowned species of cabbage known, by all Dutch epicures, by the name of the Governor's Head, and which is to this day the glory of Communipaw.

On the other hand, the shoe of Peter Stuyvesant being thrown into the river, in front of the house, gradually hardened and concreted, and became covered with barnacles, and at length turned into a gigantic oyster; being the progenitor of that illustrious species known throughout the gastronomical world by the name of the Governor's Foot.

These miracles were the salvation of Communipaw. The sages of the place immediately saw in them the hand of St. Nicholas, and understood their mystic signification. They set to work with all diligence to cultivate and multiply these great blessings; and so abundantly did the gubernatorial hat and shoe fructify and increase, that in a little time great patches of cabbages were to be seen extending from the village of Communipaw quite to the Bergen Hills; while the whole bottom of the bay in front became a vast bed of oysters. Ever since that time this excellent community has been divided into two great classes: those who cultivate the land and those who cultivate the water. The former has devoted themselves to the nurture and edification of cabbages, rearing them in all their varieties; while the latter have formed parks and plantations, under water, to which juvenile oysters are transplanted from foreign parts, to finish their education.

As these great sources of profit multiplied upon their hands, the worthy inhabitants of Communipaw began to long for a market at which to dispose of their superabundance. This gradually produced once more an intercourse with New-York; but it was always carried on by the old people and the negroes; never would they permit the young folks, of either sex, to visit the city, lest they should get tainted with foreign manners and bring home foreign fashions. Even to this day, if you see an old burgher in the market, with hat and garb of antique Dutch fashion, you may be sure he is one of the old unconquered races of the "bitter blood," who maintain their strong-hold at Communipaw.

In modern days, the hereditary bitterness against the English has lost much of its asperity, or rather has become merged in a new source of jealousy and apprehension: I allude to the incessant and wide-spreading irruptions from New-England. Word has been continually brought back to Communipaw, by those of the community who return from their trading voyages in cabbages and oysters, of the alarming power which the Yankees are gaining in the ancient city of New-Amsterdam; elbowing the genuine Knickerbockers out of all civic posts of honour and profit; bargaining them out of their hereditary homesteads; pulling down the venerable houses, with crow-step gables, which have stood since the time of the Dutch rule, and erecting, instead, granite stores, and marble banks; in a word, evincing a deadly determination to obliterate every vestige of the good old Dutch times.

In consequence of the jealousy thus awakened, the worthy traders from Communipaw confine their dealings, as much as possible, to the genuine Dutch families. If they furnish the Yankees at all, it is with inferior articles. Never can the latter procure a real "Governor's Head," or "Governor's Foot," though they have offered extravagant prices for the same, to grace their table on the annual festival of the New-England Society.

But what has carried this hostility to the Yankees to the highest pitch, was an attempt made by that all-pervading race to get possession of Communipaw itself. Yes, Sir; during the late mania for land speculation, a daring company of Yankee projectors landed before the village; stopped the honest burghers on the public highway, and endeavoured to bargain them out of their hereditary acres; displayed lithographic maps, in which their cabbage-gardens were laid out into town lots:

their oyster-parks into docks and quays; and even the House of the Four Chimneys metamorphosed into a bank, which was to enrich the whole neighbourhood with paper money.

Fortunately, the gallant Van Horn's came to the rescue, just as some of the worthy burghers were on the point of capitulating. The Yankees were put to the rout, with signal confusion, and have never since dared to show their faces in the place. The good people continue to cultivate their cabbages, and rear their oysters; they know nothing of banks, nor joint stock companies, but treasure up their money in stocking-feet, at the bottom of the family chest, or bury it in iron pots, as did their fathers and grandfathers before them.

As to the House of the Four Chimneys, it still remains in the great and tall family of the Van Horne's. Here are to be seen ancient Dutch corner cupboards, chests of drawers, and massive clothes-presses, quaintly carved, and carefully waxed and polished; together with divers thick, black-letter volumes, with brass clasps, printed of yore in Leyden and Amsterdam, and handed down from generation to generation, in the family, but never read. They are preserved in the archives, among sundry old parchment deeds, in Dutch and English, bearing the seals of the early governors of the province.

In this house, the primitive Dutch holidays of Paas and Pinxter are faithfully kept up; and New-Year celebrated with cookies and cherry-bounce; nor is the festival of the blessed St. Nicholas forgotten, when all the children are sure to hang up their stockings, and to have them filled according to their deserts; though, it is said, the good saint is occasionally perplexed in his nocturnal visits, which chimney to descend.

Of late, this portentous mansion has begun to give signs of dilapidation and decay. Some have attributed this to the visits made by the young people to the city, and their bringing thence various modern fashions; and to their neglect of the Dutch language, which is gradually becoming confined to the older persons in the community. The house, too, was greatly shaken by high winds, during the prevalence of the speculation mania, especially at the time of the landing of the Yankees. Seeing how mysteriously the fate of Communipaw is identified with this venerable mansion, we cannot wonder that the older and wiser heads of the community should be filled with dismay, whenever a brick is toppled down from one of the chimneys, or a weather-cock is blown off from a gable-end.

The present lord of this historic pile, I am happy to say, is calculated to maintain it in all its integrity. He is of patriarchal age, and is worthy of the days of the patriarchs. He has done his utmost to increase and multiply the true race in the land. His wife has not been inferior to him in zeal, and they are surrounded by a goodly progeny of children, and grand-children, and great-grand-children, who promise to perpetuate the name of Van Horne, until time shall be no more. So be it! Long may the horn of the Van Horne's continue to be exalted in the land! Tall as they are, may their shadows never be less! May the House of the Four Chimneys remain for ages, the citadel of Communipaw, and the smoke of its chimneys continue to ascend, a sweet-smelling incense in the hose of St. Nicholas!

With great respect, Mr. Editor,

Your ob't servant,

HERMANUS VANDERDONK.

Conspiracy of the Cocked Hats

TO THE EDITOR OF THE KNICKERBOCKER.

Sir,

I have read with great satisfaction the valuable paper of your correspondent, Mr. HERMANUS VANDERDONK, (who, I take it, is a descendant of the learned Adrian Vanderdonk, one of the early historians of the Nieuw-Nederlands,) giving sundry particulars, legendary and statistical, touching the venerable village of Communipaw and its fate-bound citadel, the House of the Four Chimneys. It goes to prove what I have repeatedly maintained, that we live in the midst of history and mystery and romance; and that there is no spot in the world richer in themes for the writer of historic novels, heroic melodramas, and rough-shod epics, than this same business-looking city of the Manhattoes and its environs. He who would find these elements, however, must not seek them among the modern improvements and modern people of this moneyed metropolis, but must dig for them, as for Kidd the pirate's treasures, in out-of-the-way places, and among the ruins of the past.

Poetry and romance received a fatal blow at the overthrow of the ancient Dutch dynasty, and have ever since been gradually withering under the growing domination of the Yankees. They abandoned our hearths when the old Dutch tiles were superseded by marble chimney-pieces; when brass andirons made way for polished grates, and the crackling and blazing fire of nut-wood gave place to the smoke and stench of Liverpool coal; and on the downfall of the last gable-end house, their requiem was tolled from the tower of the Dutch church in Nassau-street by the old bell that came from

Holland. But poetry and romance still live unseen among us, or seen only by the enlightened few, who are able to contemplate this city and its environs through the medium of tradition, and clothed with the associations of foregone ages.

Would you seek these elements in the country, Mr. Editor, avoid all turnpikes, rail-roads, and steamboats, those abominable inventions by which the usurping Yankees are strengthening themselves in the land, and subduing everything to utility and common-place. Avoid all towns and cities of white clapboard palaces and Grecian temples, studded with "Academics," "Seminaries," and "Institutes," which glisten along our bays and rivers; these are the strong-holds of Yankee usurpation; but if haply you light upon some rough, rambling road, winding between stone fences, Gray with moss, and overgrown with elder, poke-berry, mullein, and sweet-briar, with here and there a low, red-roofed, whitewashed farm-house, cowering among apple and cherry trees; an old stone church, with elms, willows, and button-woods, as old-looking as itself, and tombstones almost buried in their own graves; and, peradventure, a small log school-house at a cross-road, where the English is still taught with a thickness of the tongue, instead of a twang of the nose; should you, I say, light upon such a neighbourhood, Mr. Editor, you may thank your stars that you have found one of the lingering haunts of poetry and romance.

Your correspondent, Sir, has touched upon that sublime and affecting feature in the history of Communipaw, the retreat of the patriotic band of Netherlanders, led by Van Horne, whom he justly terms the Pelayo of the New-Netherlands. He has given you a picture of the manner in which they ensconced themselves in the House of the Four Chimneys, and awaited with heroic patience and perseverance the day that should see the flag of the Hogen Mogens once more floating on the fort of New-Amsterdam.

Your correspondent, Sir, has but given you a glimpse over

Rip Van Winkle and other writings

the threshold; I will now let you into the heart of the mystery of this most mysterious and eventful village.

Yes, sir, I will now--"unclasp a secret book; And to your quick conceiving discontents, I'll read you matter deep and dangerous, as full of peril and adventurous spirit, as to o'er walk a current, roaring loud, On the unsteadfast footing of a spear."

Sir, it is one of the most beautiful and interesting facts connected with the history of Communipaw, that the early feeling of resistance to foreign rule, alluded to by your correspondent, is still kept up. Yes, sir, a settled, secret, and determined conspiracy has been going on for generations among this indomitable people, the descendants of the refugees from New-Amsterdam; the object of which is to redeem their ancient seat of empire, and to drive the losel Yankees out of the land.

Communipaw, it is true, has the glory of originating this conspiracy; and it was hatched and reared in the House of the Four Chimneys; but it has spread far and wide over ancient Pavonia, surmounted the heights of Bergen, Hoboken, and Wee hawk, crept up along the banks of the Passaic and the Hackensack, until it pervades the whole chivalry of the country from Tappan Slote in the north to Piscataway in the south, including the pugnacious village of Rahway, more heroically denominated Spank-town.

Throughout all these regions a great "in-and-in confederacy" prevails, that is to say, a confederacy among the Dutch families, by dint of diligent and exclusive intermarriage, to keep the race pure and to multiply. If ever, Mr. Editor, in the course of your travels between Spank-town and Tappan Slote, you should see a cosey, low-eaved farm-house, teeming with sturdy, broad-built little urchins, you may set it down as one of the breeding places of this grand secret confederacy, stocked with the embryo deliverers of New-Amsterdam.

Washington Irving ☙53

Another step in the progress of this patriotic conspiracy, is the establishment, in various places within the ancient boundaries of the Nieuw-Nederlands, of secret, or rather mysterious associations, composed of the genuine sons of the Netherlanders, with the ostensible object of keeping up the memory of old times and customs, but with the real object of promoting the views of this dark and mighty plot, and extending its ramifications throughout the land.

Sir, I am descended from a long line of genuine Netherlanders, who, though they remained in the city of New-Amsterdam after the conquest, and throughout the usurpation, have never in their hearts been able to tolerate the yoke imposed upon them. My worthy father, who was one of the last of the cocked hats, had a little knot of cronies, of his own stamp, who used to meet in our wainscoted parlour, round a nut-wood fire, talk over old times, when the city was ruled by its native burgomasters, and groan over the monopoly of all places of power and profit by the Yankees. I well recollect the effect upon this worthy little conclave, when the Yankees first instituted then New-England Society, held their "national festival," toasted their "father land," and sang their foreign songs of triumph within the very precincts of our ancient metropolis. Sir, from that day, my father held the smell of codfish and potatoes, and the sight of pumpkin pie, in utter abomination; and whenever the annual dinner of the New-England Society came round, it was a sore anniversary for his children. He got up in an ill humour, grumbled and growled throughout the day, and not one of us went to bed that night, without having had his jacket well trounced, to the tune of "The Pilgrim Fathers."

You may judge, then, Mr. Editor, of the exaltation of all true patriots of this stamp, when the Society of Saint Nicholas was set up among us, and intrepidly established, cheek by jole, alongside of the society of the invaders. Never shall I forget the effect upon my father and his little knot of brother groaners, when tidings were brought them that the ancient banner of the Manhattoes was actually floating from the window of the City Hotel. Sir, they nearly jumped out of their silver-buckled shoes for joy. They took down their cocked hats from the pegs on which they had hanged them, as the Israelites of yore hung their harps upon the willows, in token of bondage, clapped them resolutely once more upon their heads, and cocked them in the face of every Yankee they met on the way to the banqueting-room.

The institution of this society was hailed with transport throughout the whole extent of the New-Netherlands; being considered a secret foothold gained in New-Amsterdam, and a flattering presage of future triumph. Whenever that society holds its annual feast, a sympathetic hilarity prevails throughout the land; ancient Pavonia sends over its contributions of cabbages and oysters; the House of the Four Chimneys is splendidly illuminated, and the traditional song of St. Nicholas, the mystic bond of union and conspiracy, is chaunted with closed doors, in every genuine Dutch family.

I have thus, I trust, Mr. Editor, opened your eyes to some of the grand moral, poetical, and political phenomena with which you are surrounded. You will now be able to read the "signs of the times." You will now understand what is meant by those "Knickerbocker Halls," and "Knickerbocker Hotels," and "Knickerbocker Lunches," that are daily springing up in our city and what all these "Knickerbocker Omnibuses" are driving at. You will see in them so many clouds before a storm; so many mysterious but sublime intimations of the gathering vengeance of a great though oppressed people. Above all, you will now contemplate our bay and its portentous borders, with proper feelings of awe and admiration. Talk of the Bay of Naples, and its volcanic mountains! Why, Sir, little Communipaw, sleeping among its cabbage gardens, "quiet as gunpowder," yet with this tremendous conspiracy brewing in its bosom is an object ten times as sublime (in a moral point of view, mark me) as Vesuvius in repose, though charged with lava and brimstone, and ready for an eruption.

Let me advert to a circumstance connected with this theme, which cannot but be appreciated by every heart of sensibility. You must have remarked, Mr. Editor, on summer evenings, and on Sunday afternoons, certain grave, primitive-looking personages, walking the Battery, in close confabulation, with their canes behind their backs, and ever and anon turning a wistful gaze toward the Jersey shore. These, Sir, are the sons of Saint Nicholas, the genuine Netherlanders; who regard Communipaw with pious reverence, not merely as the progenitor, but the destined regenerator, of this great metropolis. Yes, Sir; they are looking with longing eyes to the green marshes of ancient Pavonia, as did the poor conquered Spaniards of yore toward the stern mountains of Asturias, wondering whether the day of deliverance is at hand. Many is the time, when, in my boyhood, I have walked with my father and his confidential compeers on the Battery, and listened to their calculations and conjectures, and observed the points of their sharp cocked hats evermore turned toward Pavonia. Nay, Sir, I am convinced that at this moment, if I were to take down the cocked hat of my lamented father from the peg on which it has hung for years, and were to carry it to the Battery, its centre point, true as the needle to the pole, would turn to Communipaw.

Mr. Editor, the great historic drama of New-Amsterdam, is but half acted. The reigns of Walter the Doubter, William the Testy, and Peter the Headstrong, with the rise, progress, and decline of the Dutch dynasty, are but so many parts of the main action, the triumphant catastrophe of which is yet to come. Yes, Sir! the deliverance of the New-Nederland's from Yankee domination will eclipse the far-famed redemption of Spain from the Moors, and the oft-sung conquest of Granada will fade before the chivalrous triumph of New-Amsterdam.

Would that Peter Stuyvesant could rise from his grave to witness that day!

Your humble servant,

ROLOFF VAN RIPPER.

P. S. Just as I had concluded the foregoing epistle, I received a piece of intelligence, which makes me tremble for the fate of Communipaw. I fear, Mr. Editor, the grand conspiracy is in danger of being countermined and counteracted, by those all-pervading and indefatigable Yankees. Would you think it, Sir! one of them has actually affected an entry in the place by covered way; or in other words, under cover of the petticoats. Finding every other mode ineffectual, he secretly laid siege to a Dutch heiress, who owns a great cabbage-garden in her own right. Being a smooth-tongued varlet, he easily prevailed on her to elope with him, and they were privately married at Spank-town! The first notice the good people of Communipaw had of this awful event, was a lithographed map of the cabbage garden laid out in town lots, and advertised for sale! On the night of the wedding, the main weather-cock of the House of the Four Chimneys was carried away in a whirlwind! The greatest consternation reigns throughout the village!

Desultory Thoughts on Criticism

"Let a man write never so well, there are now-a-days a sort of persons they call critics, that, egad, have no more wit in them than so many hobby-horses: but they'll laugh at you, Sir, and find fault, and censure things, that, egad, I'm sure they are not able to do themselves; a sort of envious persons, that emulate the glories of persons of parts, and think to build their fame by calumniation of persons that, egad, to my knowledge, of all persons in the world, are in nature the persons that do as much despise all that, as--a--In fine, I'll say no more of 'em!" ~Rehearsal

All the world knows the story of the tempest-tossed voyager, who, coming upon a strange coast, and seeing a man hanging in chains, hailed it with joy, as the sign of a civilized country. In like manner we may hail, as a proof of the rapid advancement of civilization and refinement in this country, the increasing number of delinquent authors daily gibbeted for the edification of the public.

In this respect, as in every other, we are "going ahead" with accelerated velocity, and promising to outstrip the superannuated countries of Europe. It is really astonishing to see the number of tribunals incessantly springing up for the trial of literary offences. Independent of the high courts of Oyer and Terminer, the great quarterly reviews, we have innumerable minor tribunals, monthly and weekly, down to the Pie-poudre courts in the daily papers; insomuch that no culprit stands so little chance of escaping castigation, as an unlucky author, guilty of an unsuccessful attempt to please the public.

Seriously speaking, however, it is questionable whether our

national literature is sufficiently advanced, to bear this excess of criticism; and whether it would not thrive better, if allowed to spring up, for some time longer, in the freshness and vigour of native vegetation. When the worthy Judge Coulter, of Virginia, opened court for the first time in one of the upper counties, he was for enforcing all the rules and regulations that had grown into use in the old, long-settled counties. "This is all very well," said a shrewd old farmer; "but let me tell you, Judge Coulter, you set your coulter too deep for a new soil."

For my part, I doubt whether either writer or reader is benefited by what is commonly called criticism. The former is rendered cautious and distrustful; he fears to give way to those kindling emotions, and brave sallies of thought, which bear him up to excellence; the latter is made fastidious and cynical; or rather, he surrenders his own independent taste and judgment, and learns to like and dislike at second hand.

Let us, for a moment, consider the nature of this thing called criticism, which exerts such a sway over the literary world. The pronoun we, used by critics, has a most imposing and delusive sound. The reader pictures to himself a conclave of learned men, deliberating gravely and scrupulously on the merits of the book in question; examining it page by page, comparing and balancing their opinions, and when they have united in a conscientious verdict, publishing it for the benefit of the world: whereas the criticism is generally the crude and hasty production of an individual, scribbling to while away an idle hour, to oblige a book-seller, or to defray current expenses. How often is it the passing notion of the hour, affected by accidental circumstances; by indisposition, by peevishness, by vapours or indigestion; by personal prejudice, or party feeling. Sometimes a work is sacrificed, because the reviewer wishes a satirical article; sometimes because he wants a humorous one; and sometimes because the author reviewed has become offensively celebrated, and offers high game to the literary marksman.

Washington Irving

How often would the critic himself, if a conscientious man, reverse his opinion, had he time to revise it in a more sunny moment; but the press is waiting, the printer's devil is at his elbow; the article is wanted to make the requisite variety for the number of the review, or the author has pressing occasion for the sum he is to receive for the article, so it is sent off, all blotted and blurred; with a shrug of the shoulders, and the consolatory ejaculation: "Pshaw! curse it! it's nothing but a review!"

The critic, too, who dictates thus oracularly to the world, is perhaps some dingy, ill-favoured, ill-mannered varlet, who, were he to speak by word of mouth, would be disregarded, if not scoffed at; but such is the magic of types; such the mystic operation of anonymous writing; such the potential effect of the pronoun we, that his crude decisions, fulminated through the press, become circulated far and wide, control the opinions of the world, and give or destroy reputation.

Many readers have grown timorous in their judgments since the all-pervading currency of criticism. They fear to express a revised, frank opinion about any new work, and to relish it honestly and heartily, lest it should be condemned in the next review, and they stand convicted of bad taste. Hence, they hedge their opinions, like a gambler his bets, and leave an opening to retract, and retreat, and qualify, and neutralise every unguarded expression of delight, until their very praise declines into a faintness that is damning.

Were every one, on the contrary, to judge for himself, and speak his mind frankly and fearlessly, we should have more true criticism in the world than at present. Whenever a person is pleased with a work, he may be assured that it has good qualities. An author who pleases a variety of readers, must possess substantial powers of pleasing; or, in other words, intrinsic merits; for otherwise we acknowledge an effect, and deny the cause. The reader, therefore, should not suffer himself to be readily shaken from the conviction of his own feelings, by the sweeping censures of pseudo critics. The author he has admired, may be chargeable with a thousand faults; but it is nevertheless beauties and excellencies that have excited his admiration; and he should recollect that taste and judgment are as much evinced in the perception of beauties among defects, as in a detection of defects among beauties. For my part, I honour the blessed and blessing spirit that is quick to discover and extol all that is pleasing and meritorious. Give me the honest bee, that extracts honey from the humblest weed, but save me from the ingenuity of the spider, which traces its venom, even in the midst of a flower-garden.

If the mere fact of being chargeable with faults and imperfections is to condemn an author, who is to escape? The greatest writers of antiquity have, in this way, been obnoxious to criticism. Aristotle himself has been accused of ignorance; Aristophanes of impiety and buffoonery; Virgil of plagiarism, and a want of invention; Horace of obscurity; Cicero has been, said to want vigour and connexion, and Demosthenes to be deficient in nature, and in purity of language. Yet these have all survived the censures of the critic, and flourished on to a glorious immortality. Every now and then the world is startled by some new doctrines in matters of taste, some levelling attacks on established creeds; some sweeping denunciations of whole generations, or schools of writers, as they are called, who had seemed to be embalmed and canonized in public opinion. Such has been the case, for instance, with Pope, and Dryden, and Addison, who for a time have almost been shaken from their pedestals, and treated as false idols.

It is singular, also, to see the fickleness of the world with respect to its favourites. Enthusiasm exhausts itself, and prepares the way for dislike. The public is always for positive sentiments, and new sensations. When wearied of admiring, it delights to censure; thus, coining a double set of enjoyments out of the same subject. Scott and Byron are scarce cold in their graves, and already we find criticism beginning to call in question those powers which held the world in magic thraldom. Even in our own country, one of its greatest geniuses has had some rough passages with the censors of the press; and instantly criticism begins to unsay all that it has repeatedly said in his praise; and the public are almost led to believe that the pen which has so often delighted them, is absolutely destitute of the power to delight!

If, then, such reverses in opinion as to matters of taste can be so readily brought about, when may an author feel himself secure? Where is the anchoring-ground of popularity, when he may thus be driven from his moorings, and foundered even in harbour? The reader, too, when he is to consider himself safe in admiring, when he sees long-established altars overthrown, and his household deities dashed to the ground!

There is one consolatory reflection. Every abuse carries with it its own remedy or palliation. Thus, the excess of crude and hasty criticism, which has of late prevailed throughout the literary world, and threatened to overrun our country, begins to produce its own antidote. Where there is a multiplicity of contradictory paths, a man must make his choice; in so doing, he has to exercise his judgment, and that is one great step to mental independence. He begins to doubt all, where all differ, and but one can be in the right. He is driven to trust to his own discernment, and his natural feelings; and here he is most likely to be safe. The author, too, finding that what is condemned at one tribunal, is applauded at another, though perplexed for a time, gives way at length to the spontaneous impulse of his genius, and the dictates of his taste, and writes in the way most natural to himself. It is thus that criticism, which by its severity may have held the little world of writers in check, may, by its very excess, disarm itself of its terrors, and the hardihood of talent become restored.

G.C.

Little Britain

IN the centre of the great city of London lies a small neighbourhood, consisting of a cluster of narrow streets and courts, of very venerable and debilitated houses, which goes by the name of Little Britain. Christ Church School and St. Bartholomew's Hospital bound it on the west; Smithfield and Long Lane on the north; Aldersgate Street, like an arm of the sea, divides it from the eastern part of the city; whilst the yawning gulf of Bull-and-Mouth Street separates it from Butcher Lane, and the regions of Newgate. Over this little territory, thus bounded and designated, the great dome of St. Paul's, swelling above the intervening houses of Paternoster Row, Amen Corner, and Ave Maria Lane, looks down with an air of motherly protection.

This quarter derives its appellation from having been, in ancient times, the residence of the Dukes of Brittany. As London increased, however, rank and fashion rolled off to the west, and trade, creeping on at their heels, took possession of their deserted abodes. For some time, Little Britain became the great mart of learning, and was peopled by the busy and prolific race of booksellers; these also gradually deserted it, and, emigrating beyond the great strait of Newgate Street, settled down in Paternoster Row and St. Paul's Churchyard, where they continue to increase and multiply even at the present day.

But though thus falling into decline, Little Britain still bears traces of its former splendour. There are several houses ready to tumble down, the fronts of which are magnificently enriched with old oaken carvings of hideous faces, unknown birds, beasts, and fishes; and fruits and flowers which it would perplex a naturalist to classify. There are also, in Aldersgate Street, certain remains of what were once spacious and lordly family mansions, but which have in latter days been subdivided into several tenements. Here may often be found the family of a petty tradesman, with its trumpery furniture, burrowing among the relics of antiquated finery, in great, rambling, time-stained apartments, with fretted ceilings, gilded cornices, and enormous marble fireplaces. The lanes and courts also contain many smaller houses, not on so grand a scale, but, like your small ancient gentry, sturdily maintaining their claims to equal antiquity. These have their gable ends to the street; great bow-windows, with diamond panes set in lead, grotesque carvings, and low arched door-ways.

In this most venerable and sheltered little nest have I passed several quiet years of existence, comfortably lodged in the second floor of one of the smallest but oldest edifices. My sitting-room is an old wainscoted chamber, with small panels, and set off with a miscellaneous array of furniture. I have a particular respect for three or four high-backed claw-footed chairs, covered with tarnished brocade, which bear the marks of having seen better days, and have doubtless figured in some of the old palaces of Little Britain. They seem to me to keep together, and to look down with sovereign contempt upon their leathern-bottomed neighbours: as I have seen decayed gentry carry a high head among the plebeian society with which they were reduced to associate. The whole front of my sitting-room is taken up with a bow-window, on the panes of which are recorded the names of previous occupants for many generations, mingled with scraps of very indifferent gentlemanlike poetry, written in characters which I can scarcely decipher, and which extol the charms of many a beauty of Little Britain who has long, long since bloomed, faded, and passed away. As I am an idle personage, with no apparent occupation, and pay my bill regularly every week, I am looked upon as the only independent gentleman of the neighbourhood; and, being curious to learn the internal state of a community so apparently shut up within itself, I have managed to work my way into all the concerns and secrets of the place.

Little Britain may truly be called the heart's core of the city; the stronghold of true John Bullism. It is a fragment of London as it was in its better days, with its antiquated folks and fashions. Here flourish in great preservation many of the holiday games and customs of yore. The inhabitants most religiously eat pancakes on Shrove Tuesday, hot-cross-buns on Good Friday, and roast goose at Michaelmas; they send love-letters on Valentine's Day, burn the pope on the fifth of November, and kiss all the girls under the mistletoe at Christmas. Roast beef and plum pudding are also held in superstitious veneration, and port and sherry maintain their grounds as the only true English wines; all others being considered vile, outlandish beverages.

Little Britain has its long catalogue of city wonders, which its inhabitants consider the wonders of the world: such as the great bell of St. Paul's, which sours all the beer when it tolls; the figures that strike the hours at St. Dunstan's clock; the Monument; the lions in the Tower; and the wooden giants in Guildhall. They still believe in dreams and fortune-telling, and an old woman those lives in Bull-and-Mouth Street makes a tolerable subsistence by detecting stolen goods, and promising the girls good husbands. They are apt to be rendered uncomfortable by comets and eclipses; and if a dog howls dolefully at night, it is looked upon as a sure sign of a death in the place. There are even many ghost stories current, particularly concerning the old mansion-houses; in several of which it is said strange sights are sometimes seen. Lords and ladies, the former in full bottomed wigs, hanging sleeves, and swords, the latter in lappets, stays, hoops and brocade, have been seen walking up and down the great waste chambers, on moonlight nights; and are supposed to be the shades of the ancient proprietors in their court-dresses.

Little Britain has likewise its sages and great men. One of the most important of the former is a tall, dry old gentleman, of the name of Skymen, who keeps a small apothecary's shop. He has a cadaverous countenance, full of cavities and projections; with a brown circle round each eye, like a pair of horned spectacles. He is much thought of by the old women, who consider him a kind of conjurer, because he has two of three stuffed alligators hanging up in his shop, and several snakes in bottles. He is a great reader of almanacs and newspapers, and is much given to pore over alarming accounts of plots, conspiracies, fires, earthquakes, and volcanic eruptions; which last phenomena he considers as signs of the times. He has always some dismal tale of the kind to deal out to his customers, with their doses; and thus, at the same time puts both soul and body into an uproar. He is a great believer in omens and predictions; and has the prophecies of Robert Nixon and Mother Shipton by heart. No man can make so much out of an eclipse, or even an unusually dark day; and he shook the tail of the last comet over the heads of his customers and disciples until they were nearly frightened out of their wits. He has lately got hold of a popular legend or prophecy, on which he has been unusually eloquent. There has been a saying current among the ancient sibyls, who treasure up these things, that when the grasshopper on the top of the Exchange shook hands with the dragon on the top of Bow Church Steeple, fearful events would take place. This strange conjunction, it seems, has as strangely come to pass. The same architect has been engaged lately on the repairs of the cupola of the Exchange, and the steeple of Bow church; and, fearful to relate, the dragon and the grasshopper actually lie, cheek by jole, in the yard of his workshop.

"Others," as Mr. Skryme is accustomed to say, "may go stargazing, and look for conjunctions in the heavens, but here is a conjunction on the earth, near at home, and under our own eyes, which surpasses all the signs and calculations of astrologers." Since these portentous weathercocks have thus laid their heads together, wonderful events had already occurred. The good old king, notwithstanding that he had lived eighty-two years, had all at once given up the ghost; another king had mounted the throne; a royal duke had died suddenly, --another, in France, had been murdered; there had been radical meetings in all parts of the kingdom; the bloody scenes at Manchester; the great plot of Cato Street; and above all, the queen had returned to England! All these sinister events are recounted by Mr. Skryme, with a mysterious look, and a dismal shake of the head; and being taken with his drugs, and associated in the minds of his auditors with stuffed sea-monsters, bottled serpents, and his own visage, which is a title-page of tribulation, they have spread great gloom through the minds of the people of Little Britain. They shake their heads whenever they go by Bow Church, and observe, that they never expected any good to come of taking down that steeple, which in old times told nothing but glad tidings, as the history of Whittington and his Cat bear's witness.

The rival oracle of Little Britain is a substantial cheesemonger, who lives in a fragment of one of the old family mansions, and is as magnificently lodged as a round-bellied mite in the midst of one of his own Cheshire's. Indeed, he is a man of no little standing and importance; and his renown extends through Hugging Lane, and Lad Lane, and even unto Aldermanbury. His opinion is very much taken in affairs of state, having read the Sunday papers for the last half century, together with the "Gentleman's Magazine," Rapin's "History of England," and the "Naval Chronicle." His head is stored with invaluable maxims which have borne the test of time and use for centuries. It is his firm opinion that "it is a moral impossible," so long as England is true to herself, that anything can shake her; and he has much to say on the subject of the national debt, which, somehow or other, he proves to be a great national bulwark and blessing. He passed the greater part of his life in the purlieus of Little Britain, until of late years, when, having become rich, and grown into the dignity of a Sunday cane, he begins to take his pleasure and see the world. He has therefore made several excursions to Hampstead, Highgate, and other neighbouring towns, where he has passed whole afternoons in looking back upon the metropolis through a telescope, and endeavouring to descry the steeple of St. Bartholomew's. Not a stage-coachman of Bull-and-Mouth Street but touches his hat as he passes; and he is considered quite a patron at the coach-office of the Goose and Gridiron, St. Paul's churchyard. His family have been very urgent for him to make an expedition to Margate, but he has great doubts of those new gimcracks, the steamboats, and indeed thinks himself too advanced in life to undertake sea-voyages.

Little Britain has occasionally its factions and divisions, and party spirit ran very high at one time in consequence of two rival "Burial Societies" being set up in the place. One held its meeting at the Swan and Horse Shoe, and was patronized by the cheesemonger; the other at the Cock and Crown, under the auspices of the apothecary; it is needless to say that the latter was the most flourishing. I have passed an evening or two at each, and have acquired much valuable information, as to the best mode of being buried, the comparative merits of churchyards, together with diver's hints on the subject of patent-iron coffins. I have heard the question discussed in all its bearings as to the legality of prohibiting the latter on account of their durability. The feuds occasioned by these societies have happily died of late; but they were for a long-time prevailing theme of controversy, the people of Little Britain being extremely solicitous of funereal honours and of lying comfortably in their graves.

Besides these two funeral societies there is a third of quite a different cast, which tends to throw the sunshine of good-humour over the whole neighbourhood. It meets once a week at a little old-fashioned house, kept by a jolly publican of the name of Wagstaff, and bearing for insignia a resplendent half-moon, with a most seductive bunch of grapes. The old edifice is covered with inscriptions to catch the eye of the thirsty wayfarer, such as "Truman, Hanbury, and Co.'s Entire," "Wine, Rum, and Brandy Vaults," "Old Tom, Rum and Compounds, etc." This indeed has been a temple of Bacchus and Momus from time immemorial. It has always been in the family of the Wagstaff's, so that its history is tolerably preserved by the present landlord. It was much frequented by the gallants and cavalieros of the reign of Elizabeth, and was looked into now and then by the wits of Charles the Second's Day. But what Wagstaff principally prides himself upon is, that Henry the Eighth, in one of his nocturnal rambles, broke the head of one of his ancestors with his famous walking-staff. This, however, is considered as a rather dubious and vainglorious boast of the landlord.

The club which now holds its weekly sessions here goes by the name of "The Roaring Lads of Little Britain." They abound in old catches, glees, and choice stories, that are traditional in the place, and not to be met with in any other part of the metropolis. There is a madcap undertaker who is inimitable at a merry song; but the life of the club, and indeed the prime wit of Little Britain, is bully Wagstaff himself. His ancestors were all wags before him, and he has inherited with the inn a large stock of songs and jokes, which go with it from generation to generation as heirlooms. He is a dapper little fellow, with bandy legs and pot belly, a red face, with a moist, merry eye, and a little shock of gray hair behind. At the opening of every club night, he is called in to sing his "Confession of Faith," which is the famous old drinking trawl from "Gammer Gurton's Needle." He sings it, to be sure, with many variations, as he received it from his father's lips; for it has been a standing favourite at the Half-Moon and Bunch of Grapes ever since it was written; nay, he affirms that his predecessors have often had the honour of singing it before the nobility and gentry at

Christmas mummeries, when Little Britain was in all its glory.

It would do one's heart good to hear, on a club night, the shouts of merriment, the snatches of song, and now and then the choral bursts of half a dozen discordant voices, which issue from this jovial mansion. At such times the street is lined with listeners, who enjoy a delight equal to that of gazing into a confectioner's window, or snuffing up the steams of a cookshop.

There are two annual events which produce great stir and sensation in Little Britain; these are St. Bartholomew's Fair, and the Lord Mayor's Day. During the time of the fair, which is held in the adjoining regions of Smithfield, there is nothing going on but gossiping and gadding about. The late quiet streets of Little Britain are overrun with an eruption of strange figures and faces; every tavern is a scene of rout and revel. The fiddle and the song are heard from the tap-room, morning, noon, and night; and at each window may be seen some group of boon companions, with half-shut eyes, hats on one side, pipe in mouth, and tankard in hand, fondling, and prosing, and singing maudlin songs over their liquor. Even the sober decorum of private families, which I must say is rigidly kept up at other times among my neighbours, is no proof against this Saturnalia. There is no such thing as keeping maid-servants within doors. Their brains are absolutely set madding with Punch and the Puppet Show; the Flying Horses; Signior Polito; the Fire-Eater; the celebrated Mr. Paap; and the Irish Giant. The children, too, lavish all their holiday money in toys and gilt gingerbread, and fill the house with the Lilliputian din of drums, trumpets, and penny whistles.

But the Lord mayor's Day is the great anniversary. The Lord Mayor is looked up to by the inhabitants of Little Britain as the greatest potentate upon earth; his gilt coach with six horses as the summit of human splendour; and his procession, with all the Sheriffs and Aldermen in his train, as the grandest of earthly pageants. How they exult in the idea that the King himself dare not enter the city without first knocking at the gate of Temple Bar, and asking permission of the Lord Mayor: for if he did, heaven and earth! there is no knowing what might be the consequence. The man in Armor, who rides before the Lord mayor, and is the city champion, has orders to cut down everybody that offends against the dignity of the city; and then there is the little man with a velvet porringer on his head, who sits at the window of the state-coach, and holds the city sword, as long as a pike-staff--Odd's blood! If he once draws that sword, Majesty itself is not safe!

Under the protection of this mighty potentate, therefore, the good people of Little Britain sleep in peace. Temple Bar is an effectual barrier against all interior foes; and as to foreign invasion, the Lord Mayor has but to throw himself into the Tower, call in the trainbands, and put the standing army of Beef-eaters under arms, and he may bid defiance to the world!

Thus, wrapped up in its own concerns, its own habits, and its own opinions, Little Britain has long flourished as a sound heart to this great fungous metropolis. I have pleased myself with considering it as a chosen spot, where the principles of sturdy John Bullism were garnered up, like seed corn, to renew the national character, when it had run to waste and degeneracy. I have rejoiced also in the general spirit of harmony that prevailed throughout it; for though there might now and then be a few clashes of opinion between the adherents of the cheesemonger and the apothecary, and an occasional feud between the burial societies, yet these were but transient clouds, and soon passed away. The neighbours met with good-will, parted with a shake of the hand, and never abused each other except behind their backs.

I could give rare descriptions of snug junketing parties at which I have been present; where we played at All-fours, Pope-Joan, Tome-come-tickle-me, and other choice old games; and where we sometimes had a good old English country dance to the tune of Sir Roger de Coverley. Once a year, also, the neighbours would gather together, and go on a gypsy party to Epping Forest. It would have done any man's heart good to see the merriment that took place here as we banqueted on the grass under the trees. How we made the woods ring with bursts of laughter at the songs of little Wagstaff and the merry undertaker! After dinner, too, the young folks would play at blind-man's-buff and hide-and-seek; and it was amusing to see them tangled among the briers, and to hear a fine romping girl now and then squeak from among the bushes. The elder folks would gather round the cheesemonger and the apothecary to hear them talk politics; for they generally brought out a newspaper in their pockets, to pass away time in the country. They would now and then, to be sure, get a little warm in argument; but their disputes were always adjusted by reference to a worthy old umbrella maker, in a double chin, who, never exactly comprehending the subject, managed somehow or other to decide in favour of both parties.

All empires, however, says some philosopher or historian, are doomed to changes and revolutions. Luxury and innovation creep in; factions arise; and families now and then spring up, whose ambition and intrigues throw the whole system into confusion. Thus, in latter days has the tranquillity of Little Britain been grievously disturbed, and its golden simplicity of manners threatened with total subversion by the aspiring family of a retired butcher.

The family of the Lambs had long been among the most thriving and popular in the neighbourhood; the Miss Lambs were the belles of Little Britain, and everybody was pleased when Old Lamb had made money enough to shut up shop, and put his name on a brass plate on his door. In an evil hour, however, one of the Miss Lambs had the honour of being a lady in attendance on the Lady Mayoress, at her grand annual ball, on which occasion she wore three towering ostrich feathers on her head. The family never got over it; they were immediately smitten with a passion for high life; set up a one-horse carriage, put a bit of gold lace round the errand boy's hat, and have been the talk and detestation of the whole neighbourhood ever since. They could no longer be induced to play at Pope-Joan or blind-man's-buff; they could endure no dances but quadrilles, which nobody had ever heard of in Little Britain; and they took to reading novels, talking bad French, and playing upon the piano. Their brother, too, who had been articled to an attorney, set up for a dandy and a critic, characters hitherto unknown in these parts; and he confounded the worthy folks exceedingly by talking about Kean, the opera, and the "Edinburgh Review."

What was still worse, the Lambs gave a grand ball, to which they neglected to invite any of their old neighbours; but they had a great deal of genteel company from Theobald's Road, Red-Lion Square, and other parts towards the west. There were several beaux of their brother's acquaintance from Gray's Inn Lane and Hatton Garden; and not less than three Aldermen's ladies with their daughters. This was not to be forgotten or forgiven. All Little Britain was in an uproar with the smacking of whips, the lashing of miserable horses, and the rattling and the jingling of hackney coaches. The gossips of the neighbourhood might be seen popping their nightcaps out at every window, watching the crazy vehicles rumble by; and there was a knot of virulent old cronies, that kept a lookout from a house just opposite the retired butchers, and scanned and criticised every one that knocked at the door.

This dance was a cause of almost open war, and the whole neighbourhood declared they would have nothing more to say to the Lambs. It is true that Mrs. Lamb, when she had no engagements with her quality acquaintance, would give little humdrum tea-junketings to some of her old cronies, "quiet," as she would say, "in a friendly way;" and it is equally true that her invitations were always accepted, in spite of all previous vows to the contrary. Nay, the good ladies would sit and be delighted with the music of the Miss Lambs, who would condescend to strum an Irish melody for them on the piano; and they would listen with wonderful interest to Mrs. Lamb's anecdotes of Alderman Plunket's family, of Ports Kenward, and the Miss Timberlake's, the rich heiresses of Crutched-Friars; but then they relieved their consciences, and averted the reproaches of their confederates, by canvassing at the next gossiping convocation everything that had passed, and pulling the Lambs and their rout all to pieces.

The only one of the family that could not be made fashionable was the retired butcher himself. Honest Lamb, in spite of the meekness of his name, was a rough, hearty old fellow, with the voice of a lion, a head of black hair like a shoe-brush, and a broad face mottled like his own beef. It was in vain that the daughters always spoke of him as "the old gentleman," addressed him as "papa," in tones of infinite softness, and endeavoured to coax him into a dressing-gown and slippers, and other gentlemanly habits. Do what they might, there was no keeping down the butcher. His sturdy nature would break through all their glozing's. He had a hearty vulgar good-humour that was irrepressible. His very jokes made his sensitive daughters' shudder; and he persisted in wearing his blue cotton coat of a morning, dining at two o'clock, and having a "bit of sausage with his tea."

He was doomed, however, to share the unpopularity of his family. He found his old comrades gradually growing cold and civil to him; no longer laughing at his jokes; and now and then throwing out a fling at "some people," and a hint about "quality binding." This both nettled and perplexed the honest butcher; and his wife and daughters, with the consummate policy of the shrewder sex, taking advantage of the circumstance, at length prevailed upon him to give up his afternoon's pipe and tankard at Wagstaff's; to sit after dinner by himself, and take his pint of port--a liquor he detested--and to nod in his chair in solitary and dismal gentility.

The Miss Lambs might now be seen flaunting along the streets in French bonnets, with unknown beaux; and talking and laughing so loud that it distressed the nerves of every good lady within hearing. They even went so far as to attempt patronage, and actually induced a French dancing-master to set up in the neighbourhood; but the worthy folks of Little Britain took fire at it, and did so persecute the poor Gaul that he was fain to pack up fiddle and dancing-pumps, and decamp with such precipitation that he absolutely forgot to pay for his lodgings.

I had flattered myself, at first, with the idea that all this fiery indignation on the part of the community was merely the overflowing of their zeal for good old English manners, and their horror of innovation; and I applauded the silent contempt they were so vociferous in expressing, for upstart pride, French fashions, and the Miss Lambs. But I grieve to say that I soon perceived the infection had taken hold; and that my neighbours, after condemning, were beginning to follow their example. I overheard my landlady importuning her husband to let their daughters have one quarter at French and music, and that they might take a few lessons in quadrille. I even saw, in the course of a few Sundays, no less than five French bonnets, precisely like those of the Miss Lambs, parading about Little Britain.

I still had my hopes that all this folly would gradually die away; that the Lambs might move out of the neighbourhood; might die, or might run away with attorneys' apprentices; and that quiet and simplicity might be again restored to the community. But unluckily a rival power arose. An opulent oilman died, and left a widow with a large jointure and a family of buxom daughters. The young ladies had long been repining in secret at the parsimony of a prudent father, which kept down all their elegant aspiring. Their ambition, being now no longer restrained, broke out into a blaze, and they openly took the field against the family of the butcher. It is true that the Lambs, having had the first start, had naturally an advantage of them in the fashionable career. They could speak a little bad French, play the piano, dance quadrilles, and had formed high acquaintances; but the Trotters were not to be distanced. When the Lambs appeared with two feathers in their hats, the Miss Trotters mounted four, and of twice as fine colours. If the Lambs gave a dance, the Trotters were sure not to be behindhand: and though they might not boast of as good company, yet they had double the number, and were twice as merry.

The whole community has at length divided itself into fashionable factions, under the banners of these two families. The old games of Pope-Joan and Tom-come-tickle-me are entirely discarded; there is no such thing as getting up an honest country dance; and on my attempting to kiss a young lady under the mistletoe last Christmas, I was indignantly repulsed; the Miss Lambs having pronounced it "shocking vulgar." Bitter rivalry has also broken out as to the most fashionable part of Little Britain; the Lambs standing up for the dignity of the Cross-Keys Square, and the Trotters for the vicinity of St. Bartholomew's.

Thus is this little territory torn by factions and internal dissensions, like the great empire who name it bears; and what will be the result would puzzle the apothecary himself, with all his talent at prognostics, to determine; though I apprehend that it will terminate in the total downfall of genuine John Bullism.

The immediate effects are extremely unpleasant to me. Being a single man, and, as I observed before, rather an idle good-for-nothing personage, I have been considered the only gentleman by profession in the place. I stand therefore in high favour with both parties, and have to hear all their cabinet councils and mutual backbiting's. As I am too civil not to agree with the ladies on all occasions, I have committed myself most horribly with both parties, by abusing their opponents. I might manage to reconcile this to my conscience, which is a truly accommodating one, but I cannot to my apprehension- -if the Lambs and Trotters ever come to a reconciliation, and compare notes, I am ruined!

I have determined, therefore, to beat a retreat in time, and am actually looking out for some other nest in this great city, where old English manners are still kept up; where French is neither eaten, drunk, danced, nor spoken; and where there are no fashionable families of retired tradesmen. This found, I will, like a veteran rat, hasten away before I have an old house about my ears; bid a long, though a sorrowful, adieu to my present abode, and leave the rival factions of the Lambs and the Trotters to divide the distracted empire of Little Britain.

National Nomenclature

Sir,

I am somewhat of the same way of thinking, in regard to names, with that profound philosopher, Mr. Shandy, the elder, who maintained that some inspired high thoughts and heroic aims, while others entailed irretrievable meanness and vulgarity; insomuch that a man might sink under the insignificance of his name, and be absolutely "Nicodemus Ed into nothing." I have ever, therefore, thought it a great hardship for a man to be obliged to struggle through life with some ridiculous or ignoble Christian name, as it is too often falsely called, inflicted on him in infancy, when he could not choose for himself; and would give him free liberty to change it for one more to his taste, when he had arrived at years of discretion.

I have the same notion with respect to local names. Some at once prepossess us in favour of a place; others repel us, by unlucky associations of the mind; and I have known scenes worthy of being the very haunt of poetry and romance, yet doomed to irretrievable vulgarity, by some ill-chosen name, which not even the magic numbers of a Halleck or a Bryant could elevate into poetical acceptation.

This is an evil unfortunately too prevalent throughout our country. Nature has stamped the land with features of sublimity and beauty; but some of our noblest mountains and loveliest streams are in danger of remaining for ever unhonored and unsung, from bearing appellations totally abhorrent to the Muse. In the first place, our country is deluged with names taken from places in the old world, and applied to places having no possible affinity or resemblance to their namesakes. This betokens a forlorn poverty of invention, and a second-hand spirit, content to cover its nakedness with borrowed or cast-off clothes of Europe.

Then we have a shallow affectation of scholarship: the whole catalogue of ancient worthies is shaken out from the back of Lempriere's Classical Dictionary, and a wide region of wild country sprinkled over with the names of the heroes, poets, and sages of antiquity, jumbled into the most whimsical juxtaposition. Then we have our political god-fathers; topographical engineers, perhaps, or persons employed by government to survey and lay out townships. These, forsooth, glorify the patrons that give them bread; so, we have the names of the great official men of the day scattered over the land, as if they were the real "salt of the earth," with which it was to be seasoned. Well for us is it, when these official great men happen to have names of fair acceptation; but wo unto us, should a Tubbs or a Potts be in power: we are sure, in a little while, to find Tubbsvilles and Pottsylvanias springing up in every direction.

Under these melancholy dispensations of taste and loyalty, therefore, Mr. Editor, it is with a feeling of dawning hope, that I have lately perceived the attention of persons of intelligence beginning to be awakened on this subject. I trust if the matter should once be taken up, it will not be readily abandoned. We are yet young enough, as a country, to remedy and reform much of what has been done, and to release many of our rising towns and cities, and our noble streams, from names calculated to vulgarize the land.

I have, on a former occasion, suggested the expediency of searching out the original Indian names of places, and wherever they are striking and euphonious, and those by which they have been superseded are glaringly objectionable, to restore them. They would have the merit of originality, and of belonging to the country; and they would remain as reliques of the native lords of the soil, when every other vestige had disappeared. Many of these names may easily be regained, by reference to old title deeds, and to the archives of states and counties. In my own case, by examining the records of the county clerk's office, I have discovered the Indian names of various places and objects in the neighbourhood, and have found them infinitely superior to the trite, poverty-stricken names which had been given by the settlers. A beautiful pastoral stream, for instance, which winds for many a mile through one of the loveliest little valleys in the state, has long been known by the common-place name of the "Saw-mill River." In the old Indian grants, it is designated as the Neper an. Another, a perfectly wizard stream, which winds through the wildest recesses of Sleepy Hollow, bears the hum-drum name of Mill Creek: in the Indian grants, it sustains the euphonious title of the Pocantico.

Similar researches have released Long-Island from many of those paltry and vulgar names which fringed its beautiful shores; their Cow Bays, and Cow Necks, and Oyster Ponds, and Mosquito Coves, which spread a spell of vulgarity over the whole island, and kept persons of taste and fancy at a distance.

It would be an object worthy the attention of the historical societies, which are springing up in various parts of the Union, to have maps executed of their respective states or neighbourhoods, in which all the Indian local names should, as far as possible, be restored. In fact, it appears to me that the nomenclature of the country is almost of sufficient importance for the foundation of a distinct society; or rather, a corresponding association of persons of taste and judgment, of all parts of the Union. Such an association, if properly constituted and composed, comprising especially all the literary talent of the country, though it might not have legislative power in its enactments, yet would have the all-pervading power of the press; and the changes in nomenclature which it might dictate, being at once adopted by elegant writers in prose and poetry, and interwoven with the literature of the country, would ultimately pass into popular currency.

Should such a reforming association arise, I beg to recommend to its attention all those mongrel names that have the adjective New prefixed to them, and pray they may be one and all kicked out of the country. I am for none of these second-hand appellations, that stamp us a second-hand people, and that are to perpetuate us a new country to the end of time. Odds my life! Mr. Editor, I hope and trust we are to live to be an old nation, as well as our neighbours, and have no idea that our cities, when they shall have attained to venerable antiquity, shall still be dubbed New-York, and New-London, and new this and new that, like the Pont-Neuf, (the New Bridge,) at Paris, which is the oldest bridge in that capital, or like the Vicar of Wakefield's horse, which continued to be called "the colt," until he died of old age.

Speaking of New-York, reminds me of some observations which I met with some time since, in one of the public papers, about the name of our state and city. The writer proposes to substitute for the present names, those of the State of Ontario, and the CITY OF MANHATTAN. I concur in his suggestion most heartily. Though born and brought up in the city of New-York, and though I love every stick and stone about it, yet I do not, nor ever did, relish its name. I like neither its sound nor its significance. As to its significance, the very adjective new gives to our great commercial metropolis a second-hand character, as if referring to some older, more dignified, and important place, of which it was a mere copy; though in fact, if I am rightly informed, the whole name commemorates a grant by Charles II. to his brother, the duke of York, made in the spirit of royal munificence, of a tract of country which did not belong to him. As to the sound, what can you make of it, either in poetry or prose? New-York! Why, Sir, if it were to share the fate of Troy itself; to suffer a ten years' siege, and be sacked and plundered; no modern Homer would ever be able to elevate the name to epic dignity.

Now, Sir, ONTARIO would be a name worthy of the empire state. It bears with it the majesty of that internal sea which washes our north western shore. Or, if any objection should be made, from its not being completely embraced within our boundaries, there is the MOHEGAN, one of the Indian names for that glorious river, the Hudson, which would furnish an excellent state appellation. So also New-York might be called Manhattan, as it is named in some of the early records, and Manhattan used as the adjective. Manhattan, however, stands well as a substantive, and "Manhattanese," which I observe Mr. COOPER has adopted in some of his writings, would be a very good appellation for a citizen of the commercial metropolis.

A word or two more, Mr. Editor, and I have done. We want a NATIONAL NAME. We want it poetically, and we want it politically. With the poetical necessity of the case, I shall not trouble myself. I leave it to our poets to tell how they manage to steer that collocation of words, "The United States of North America," down the swelling tide of song, and to float the whole raft out upon the sea of heroic poesy. I am now speaking of the mere purposes of common life. How is a citizen of this republic to designate himself? As an American? There are two Americas, each subdivided into various empires, rapidly rising in importance. As a citizen of the United States? It is a clumsy, lumbering title, yet still it is not distinctive; for we have now the United States of Central America; and heaven knows how many "United States" may spring up under the Proteus changes of Spanish America.

This may appear matter of small concernment; but any one that has travelled in foreign countries must be conscious of the embarrassment and circumlocution sometimes occasioned by the want of a perfectly distinct and explicit national appellation. In France, when I have announced myself as an American, I have been supposed to belong to one of the French colonies; in Spain, to be from Mexico, or Peru, or some other Spanish-American country. Repeatedly have I found myself involved in a long geographical and political definition of my national identity.

Now, Sir, meaning no disrespect to any of our co-heirs of this great quarter of the world, I am for none of this coparceny in a name that is to mingle us up with the riff-raff colonies and off-sets of every nation of Europe. The title of American may serve to tell the quarter of the world to which I belong, the same as a Frenchman or an Englishman may call himself a European; but I want my own peculiar national name to rally under. I want an appellation that shall tell at once, and in a way not to be mistaken, that I belong to this very portion of America, geographical and political, to which it is my pride and happiness to belong; that I am of the Anglo-Saxon race which founded this Anglo-Saxon empire in the wilderness; and that I have no part or parcel with any other race or empire, Spanish, French, or Portuguese, in either of the Americas. Such an appellation, Sir, would have magic in it. It would bind every part of the confederacy together as with a keystone; it would be a passport to the citizen of our republic throughout the world.

We have it in our power to furnish ourselves with such a national appellation, from one of the grand and eternal features of our country; from that noble chain of mountains which formed its back-bone, and ran through the "old confederacy," when it first declared our national independence. I allude to the Appalachian or Alleghany mountains. We might do this without any very inconvenient change in our present titles. We might still use the phrase, "The United States," substituting Appalachia, or Alleghania, (I should prefer the latter,) in place of America. The title of Appalachian, or Alleghanian, would still announce us as Americans, but would specify us as citizens of the Great Republic. Even our old national cypher of U. S. A. might remain unaltered, designating the United States of Alleghania.

These are crude ideas, Mr. Editor, hastily thrown out to elicit the ideas of others, and to call attention to a subject of more national importance than may at first be supposed.

Very respectfully yours,

Geoffrey Crayon.

Pelayo and the Merchant's Daughter

BY THE AUTHOR OF THE SKETCH-BOOK.

It is the common lamentation of Spanish historiographers, that, for an obscure and melancholy space of time immediately succeeding the conquest of their country by the Moslems, its history is a mere wilderness of dubious facts, groundless fables, and rash exaggerations. Learned men, in cells and cloisters, have worn out their lives in vainly endeavouring to connect incongruous events, and to account for startling improbabilities, recorded of this period. The worthy Jesuit, Padre Abarca, declares that, for more than forty years during which he had been employed in theological controversies, he had never found any so obscure and inexplicable as those which rise out of this portion of Spanish history, and that the only fruit of an indefatigable, prolix, and even prodigious study of the subject, was a melancholy and mortifying state of indecision.

[Footnote: PADRE PEDRO ABARCA. Anales de Aragon, Anti Regno, F2.]

During this apocryphal period, flourished PELAYO, the deliverer of Spain, whose name, like that of William Wallace, will ever be linked with the glory of his country, but linked, in like manner, by a bond in which fact and fiction are inextricably interwoven.

The quaint old chronicle of the Moor Rasis, which, though wild and fanciful in the extreme, is frequently drawn upon for early facts by Spanish historians, professes to give the birth, parentage, and whole course of fortune of Pelayo, without the least doubt or hesitation. It makes him a son of the Duke of Cantabria, and descended, both by father and mother's side, from the Gothic kings of Spain. I shall pass over the romantic story of his childhood, and shall content myself with a scene of his youth, which was spent in a castle among the Pyrenees, under the eye of his widowed and noble-minded mother, who caused him to be instructed in everything befitting a cavalier of gentle birth. While the sons of the nobility were revelling amid the pleasures of a licentious court, and sunk in that vicious and effeminate indulgence which led to the perdition of unhappy Spain, the youthful Pelayo, in his rugged mountain school, was steeled to all kinds of hardy exercise. A great part of his time was spent in hunting the bears, the wild boars, and the wolves, with which the Pyrenees abounded; and so purely and chastely was he brought up, by his good lady mother, that, if the ancient chronicle from which I draw my facts may be relied on, he had attained his one-and-twentieth year, without having once sighed for woman!

Nor were his hardy contests confined to the wild beasts of the forest. Occasionally he had to contend with adversaries of a more formidable character. The skirts and defiles of these border mountains were often infested by marauders from the Gallic plains of Gascony. The Gascons, says an old chronicler, were a people who used smooth words when expedient, but force when they had power, and were ready to lay their hands on everything they met. Though poor, they were proud; for there was not one who did not pride himself on being a hijo-dalgo, or the son of somebody.

At the head of a band of these needy hijodalgos of

Gascony, was one Arnaud, a broken-down cavalier. He and four of his followers were well armed and mounted; the rest were a set of scamper-grounds on foot, furnished with darts and javelins. They were the terror of the border; here to-day and gone to-morrow; sometimes in one pass, sometimes in another. They would make sudden inroads into Spain, scour the roads, plunder the country, and were over the mountains and far away before a force could be collected to pursue them.

Now it happened one day, that a wealthy burgher of Bordeaux, who was a merchant, trading with Biscay, set out on a journey for that province. As he intended to sojourn there for a season, he took with him his wife, who was a goodly dame, and his daughter, a gentle damsel, of marriageable age, and exceeding fair to look upon. He was attended by a trusty clerk from his comptoir, and a man servant; while another servant led a hackney, laden with bags of money, with which he intended to purchase merchandise.

When the Gascons heard of this wealthy merchant and his convoy passing through the mountains, they thanked their stars, for they considered all peaceful men of traffic as lawful spoil, sent by providence for the benefit of hidalgos like themselves, of valour and gentle blood, who lived by the sword. Placing themselves in ambush, in a lonely defile, by which the travellers had to pass, they silently awaited their coming. In a little while they beheld them approaching. The merchant was a fair, portly man, in a buff surcoat and velvet cap. His looks bespoke the good cheer of his native city, and he was mounted on a stately, well-fed steed, while his wife and daughter paced gently on palfreys by his side.

The travellers had advanced some distance in the defile, when the Bandoleros rushed forth and assailed them. The merchant, though but little used to the exercise of arms, and unwieldy in his form, yet made valiant defence, having his wife and daughter and money-bags at hazard. He was wounded in

Rip Van Winkle and other writings

two places, and overpowered; one of his servants was slain, the other took to flight.

The freebooters then began to ransack for spoil, but were disappointed at not finding the wealth they had expected. Putting their swords to the breast of the trembling merchant, they demanded where he had concealed his treasure, and learned from him of the hackney that was following, laden with, money. Overjoyed at this intelligence, they bound their captives to trees, and awaited the arrival of the golden spoil.

On this same day, Pelayo was out with his huntsmen among the mountains, and had taken his stand on a rock, at a narrow pass, to await the sallying forth of a wild boar. Close by him was a page, conducting a horse, and at the saddle-bow hung his Armor, for he was always prepared for fight among these border mountains. While thus posted, the servant of the merchant came flying from the robbers. On beholding Pelayo, he fell on his knees, and implored his life, for he supposed him to be one of the bands. It was some time before he could be relieved from his terror, and made to tell his story. When Pelayo heard of the robbers, he concluded they were the crew of Gascon hidalgos, upon the scamper. Taking his Armor from the page, he put on his helmet, slung his buckler round his neck, took lance in hand, and mounting his steed, compelled the trembling servant to guide him to the scene of action. At the same time, he ordered the page to seek his huntsmen, and summon them to his assistance.

When the robbers saw Pelayo advancing through the forest, with a single attendant on foot, and beheld his rich Armor sparkling in the sun, they thought a new prize had fallen into their hands, and Arnaud and two of his companions, mounting their horses, advanced to meet him. As they approached, Pelayo stationed himself in a narrow pass between two rocks, where he could only be assailed in front, and bracing his buckler, and lowering his lance, awaited their coming.

"Who and what are ye," cried he, "and what seek ye in this land?"

"We are huntsmen," replied Arnaud, "and lo! our game runs into our toils!"

"By my faith," replied Pelayo, "thou wilt find the game more readily roused than taken: have at thee for a villain!"

So, saying, he put spurs to his horse, and ran full speed upon him. The Gascon, not expecting so sudden an attack from a single horseman, was taken by surprise. He hastily couched his lance, but it merely glanced on the shield of Pelayo, who sent his own through the middle of his breast, and threw him out of his saddle to the earth. One of the other robbers made at Pelayo, and wounded him slightly in the side, but received a blow from the sword of the latter, which cleft his skull-cap, and sank into his brain. His companion, seeing him fall, put spurs to his steed, and galloped off through the forest.

Beholding several other robbers on foot coming up, Pelayo returned to his station between the rocks, where he was assailed by them all at once. He received two of their darts on his buckler, a javelin razed his cuirass, and glancing down, wounded his horse. Pelayo then rushed forth, and struck one of the robbers dead: the others, beholding several huntsmen advancing, took to flight, but were pursued, and several of them taken.

The good merchant of Bordeaux and his family beheld this scene with trembling and amazement, for never had they looked upon such feats of arms. They considered Don Pelayo as a leader of some rival band of robbers; and when the bonds were loosed by which they were tied to the trees, they fell at his feet and implored mercy. The females were soonest undeceived, especially the daughter; for the damsel was struck with the noble countenance and gentle demeanour of Pelayo, and said to herself: "Surely nothing evil can dwell in so goodly and gracious a form."

Pelayo now sounded his horn, which echoed from rock to rock, and was answered by shouts and horns from various parts of the mountains. The merchant's heart misgave him at these signals, and especially when he beheld more than forty men gathering from glen and thicket. They were clad in hunters' dresses, and armed with boar-spears, darts, and hunting-swords, and many of them led hounds in long leashes. All this was a new and wild scene to the astonished merchant; nor were his fears abated, when he saw his servant approaching with the hackney, laden with money-bags; "for of a certainty," said he to himself, "this will be too tempting a spoil for these wild hunters of the mountains."

Pelayo, however, took no more notice of the gold than if it had been so much dross; at which the honest burgher marvelled exceedingly. He ordered that the wounds of the merchant should be dressed, and his own examined. On taking off his cuirass, his wound was found to be but slight; but his men were so exasperated at seeing his blood, that they would have put the captive robbers to instant death, had he not forbidden them to do them any harm.

The huntsmen now made a great fire at the foot of a tree, and bringing a boar which they had killed, cut off portions and roasted them, or broiled them on the coals. Then drawing forth loaves of bread from their wallets, they devoured their food half raw, with the hungry relish of huntsmen and mountaineers. The merchant, his wife, and daughter, looked at all this, and wondered, for they had never beheld so savage a repast.

Pelayo then inquired of them if they did not desire to eat; they were too much in awe of him to decline, though they felt a loathing at the thought of partaking of this hunter's fare; but he ordered a linen cloth to be spread under the shade of a great oak, on the grassy margin of a clear running stream;

and to their astonishment, they were served, not with the flesh of the boar, but with dainty cheer, such as the merchant had scarcely hoped to find out of the walls of his native city of Bordeaux.

The good burgher was of a community renowned for gastronomic prowess: his fears having subsided, his appetite was now awakened, and he addressed himself manfully to the viands that were set before him. His daughter, however, could not eat: her eyes were ever and anon stealing to gaze on Pelayo, whom she regarded with gratitude for his protection, and admiration for his valour; and now that he had laid aside his helmet, and she beheld his lofty countenance, glowing with manly beauty, she thought him something more than mortal. The heart of the gentle donzella, says the ancient chronicler, was kind and yielding; and had Pelayo thought fit to ask the greatest boon that love and beauty could bestow--doubtless meaning her fair hand--she could not have had the cruelty to tell him nay. Pelayo, however, had no such thoughts: the love of woman had never yet entered his heart; and though he regarded the damsel as the fairest maiden he had ever beheld, her beauty caused no perturbation in his breast.

When the repast was over, Pelayo offered to conduct the merchant and his family through the defiles of the mountains, lest they should be molested by any of the scattered band of robbers. The bodies of the slain marauders were buried, and the corpse of the servant was laid upon one of the horses captured in the battle. Having formed their cavalcade, they pursued their way slowly up one of the steep and winding passes of the Pyrenees.

Toward sunset, they arrived at the dwelling of a holy hermit. It was hewn out of the living rock; there was a cross over the door, and before it was a great spreading oak, with a sweet spring of water at its foot. The body of the faithful servant who had fallen in the defence of his lord, was buried close by the wall of this sacred retreat, and the hermit promised to perform masses for the repose of his soul. Then Pelayo obtained from the holy father consent that the merchant's wife and daughter should pass the night within his cell; and the hermit made beds of moss for them, and gave them his benediction; but the damsel found little rest, so much were her thoughts occupied by the youthful champion who had rescued her from death or dishonour.

Pelayo, however, was visited by no such wandering of the mind; but, wrapping himself in his mantle, slept soundly by the fountain under the tree. At midnight, when everything was buried in deep repose, he was awakened from his sleep and beheld the hermit before him, with the beams of the moon shining upon his silver hair and beard.

"This is no time," said the latter, "to be sleeping; arise and listen to my words, and hear of the great work for which thou art chosen!"

Then Pelayo arose and seated himself on a rock, and the hermit continued his discourse.

"Behold," said he, "the ruin of Spain is at hand! It will be delivered into the hands of strangers, and will become a prey to the spoiler. Its children will be slain or carried into captivity; or such as may escape these evils, will harbour with the beasts of the forest or the eagles of the mountain. The thorn and bramble will spring up where now are seen the cornfield, the vine, and the olive; and hungry wolves will roam in place of peaceful flocks and herds. But thou, my son! tarry not thou to see these things, for thou canst not prevent them. Depart on a pilgrimage to the sepulchre of our blessed Lord in Palestine; purify thyself by prayer; enrol thyself in the order of chivalry, and prepare for the great work of the redemption of thy country; for to thee it will be given to raise it from the depth of its affliction."

Pelayo would have inquired farther into the evils thus

foretold, but the hermit rebuked his curiosity.

"Seek not to know more," said he, "than heaven is pleased to reveal. Clouds and darkness cover its designs, and prophecy is never permitted to lift up but in part the veil that rests upon the future."

The hermit ceased to speak, and Pelayo laid himself down again to take repose, but sleep was a stranger to his eyes.

When the first rays of the rising sun shone upon the tops of the mountains, the travellers assembled round the fountain beneath the tree and made their morning's repast. Then, having received the benediction of the hermit, they departed in the freshness of the day, and descended along the hollow defiles leading into the interior of Spain. The good merchant was refreshed by sleep and by his morning's meal; and when he beheld his wife and daughter thus secure by his side, and the hackney laden with his treasure close behind him, his heart was light in his bosom, and he carolled a chanson as he went, and the woodlands echoed to his song. But Pelayo rode in silence, for he revolved in his mind the portentous words of the hermit; and the daughter of the merchant ever and anon stole looks at him full of tenderness and admiration, and deep sighs betrayed the agitation of her bosom.

At length they came to the foot of the mountains, where the forests and the rocks terminated, and an open and secure country lay before the travellers. Here they halted, for their roads were widely different. When they came to part, the merchant and his wife were loud in thanks and benedictions, and the good burgher would fain have given Pelayo the largest of his sacks of gold; but the young man put it aside with a smile. "Silver and gold," said he, "need I not, but if I have deserved aught at thy hands, give me thy prayers, for the prayers of a good man are above all price."

In the meantime, the daughter had spoken never a word.

At length she raised her eyes, which were filled with tears, and looked timidly at Pelayo, and her bosom throbbed; and after a violent struggle between strong affection and virgin modesty, her heart relieved itself by words.

"Senor," said she, "I know that I am unworthy of the notice of so noble a cavalier; but suffer me to place this ring upon a finger of that hand which has so bravely rescued us from death; and when you regard it, you may consider it as a memorial of your own valour, and not of one who is too humble to be remembered by you."

With these words, she drew a ring from her finger and put it upon the finger of Pelayo; and having done this, she blushed and trembled at her own boldness, and stood as one abashed, with her eyes cast down upon the earth.

Pelayo was moved at the words of the simple maiden, and at the touch of her fair hand, and at her beauty, as she stood thus trembling and in tears before him; but as yet he knew nothing of woman, and his heart was free from the snares of love. "Amiga," (friend,) said he, "I accept thy present, and will wear it in remembrance of thy goodness;" so saying, he kissed her on the cheek.

The damsel was cheered by these words, and hoped that she had awakened some tenderness in his bosom; but it was no such thing, says the grave old chronicler, for his heart was devoted to higher and more sacred matters; yet certain it is, that he always guarded well that ring.

When they parted, Pelayo remained with his huntsmen on a cliff, watching that no evil befell them, until they were far beyond the skirts of the mountain; and the damsel often turned to look at him, until she could no longer discern him, for the distance and the tears that dimmed her eyes.

And for that he had accepted her ring, says the ancient chronicler, she considered herself wedded to him in her heart, and would never marry; nor could she be brought to look with eyes of affection upon any other man; but for the true love which she bore Pelayo, she lived and died a virgin. And she composed a book which treated of love and chivalry, and the temptations of this mortal life; and one part discoursed of celestial matters, and it was called "The Contemplations of Love;" because at the time she wrote it, she thought of Pelayo, and of his having accepted her jewel and called her by the gentle appellation of "Amiga." And often thinking of him in tender sadness, and of her never having beheld him more, she would take the book and would read it as if in his stead; and while she repeated the words of love which it contained, she would endeavour to fancy them uttered by Pelayo, and that he stood before her.

Rip Van Winkle and other writings

Recollections of The Alhambra

BY THE AUTHOR OF THE SKETCH-BOOK.

During a summer's residence in the old Moorish palace of the Alhambra, of which I have already given numerous anecdotes to the public, I used to pass much of my time in the beautiful hall of the Abencerrages, beside the fountain celebrated in the tragic story of that devoted race. Here it was, that thirty-six cavaliers of that heroic line were treacherously sacrificed, to appease the jealousy or allay the fears of a tyrant. The fountain which now throws up its sparkling jet, and sheds a dewy freshness around, ran red with the noblest blood of Granada, and a deep stain on the marble pavement is still pointed out, by the cicerones of the pile, as a sanguinary record of the massacre. I have regarded it with the same determined faith with which I have regarded the traditional stains of Rizzio's blood on the floor of the chamber of the unfortunate Mary, at Holyrood. I thank no one for endeavouring to enlighten my credulity, on such points of popular belief. It is like breaking up the shrine of the pilgrim; it is robbing a poor traveller of half the reward of his toils; for, strip travelling of its historical illusions, and what a mere fag you make of it!

For my part, I gave myself up, during my sojourn in the Alhambra, to all the romantic and fabulous traditions connected with the pile. I lived in the midst of an Arabian tale, and shut my eyes, as much as possible, to everything that called me back to every-day life; and if there is any country in Europe where one can do so, it is in poor, wild, legendary, proud-spirited, romantic Spain; where the old magnificent barbaric spirit still contends against the utilitarianism of modern civilization.

Washington Irving

In the silent and deserted halls of the Alhambra; surrounded with the insignia of regal sway, and the still vivid, though dilapidated traces of oriental voluptuousness, I was in the strong-hold of Moorish story, and everything spoke and breathed of the glorious days of Granada, when under the dominion of the crescent. When I sat in the hall of the Abencerrages, I suffered my mind to conjure up all that I had read of that illustrious line. In the proudest days of Moslem domination, the Abencerrages were the soul of everything noble and chivalrous. The veterans of the family, who sat in the royal council, were the foremost to devise those heroic enterprises, which carried dismay into the territories of the Christians; and what the sages of the family devised, the young men of the name were the foremost to execute. In all services of hazard; in all adventurous forays, and hair-breadth hazards; the Abencerrages were sure to win the brightest laurels. In those noble recreations, too, which bear so close an affinity to war; in the tilt and tourney, the riding at the ring, and the daring bull-fight; still the Abencerrages carried off the palm. None could equal them for the splendour of their array, the gallantry of their devices; for their noble bearing, and glorious horsemanship. Their open-handed munificence made them the idols of the populace, while their lofty magnanimity, and perfect faith, gained them golden opinions from the generous and high-minded. Never were they known to decry the merits of a rival, or to betray the confiding's of a friend; and the "word of an Abencerrage" was a guarantee that never admitted of a doubt.

And then their devotion to the fair! Never did Moorish beauty consider the fame of her charms established, until she had an Abencerrage for a lover; and never did an Abencerrage prove recreant to his vows. Lovely Granada! City of delights! Whoever bore the favours of thy dames more proudly on their casques, or championed them more gallantly in the chivalrous tilts of the Bivariable? Or who ever made thy moon-lit balconies, thy gardens of myrtles and roses, of oranges, citrons, and pomegranates, respond to more tender serenades?

I speak with enthusiasm on this theme; for it is connected with the recollection of one of the sweetest evenings and sweetest scenes that ever I enjoyed in Spain. One of the greatest pleasures of the Spaniards is, to sit in the beautiful summer evenings, and listen to traditional ballads, and tales about the wars of the Moors and Christians, and the "Buena's andanzas" and "grandes hechos," the "good fortunes" and "great exploits" of the hardy warriors of yore. It is worthy of remark, also, that many of these songs, or romances, as they are called, celebrate the prowess and magnanimity in war, and the tenderness and, fidelity in love, of the Moorish cavaliers, once their most formidable and hated foes. But centuries have elapsed, to extinguish the bigotry of the zealot; and the once detested warriors of Granada are now held up by Spanish poets, as the mirrors of chivalric virtue.

Such was the amusement of the evening in question. A number of us were seated in the Hall of the Abencerrages, listening to one of the most gifted and fascinating beings that I had ever met with in my wanderings. She was young and beautiful; and light and ethereal; full of fire, and spirit, and pure enthusiasm. She wore the fanciful Andalusian dress; touched the guitar with speaking eloquence; improvised with wonderful facility; and, as she became excited by her theme, or by the rapt attention of her auditors, would pour forth, in the richest and most melodious strains, a succession of couplets, full of striking description, or stirring narration, and composed, as I was assured, at the moment. Most of these were suggested by the place, and related to the ancient glories of Granada, and the prowess of her chivalry. The Abencerrages were her favourite heroes; she felt a woman's admiration of their gallant courtesy, and high-souled honour; and it was touching and inspiring to hear the praises of that generous but devoted race, chanted in this fated hall of their calamity, by the lips of Spanish beauty.

Among the subjects of which she treated, was a tale of Moslem honour, and old-fashioned Spanish courtesy, which made a strong impression on me. She disclaimed all merit of invention, however, and said she had merely dilated into verse a popular tradition; and, indeed, I have since found the main facts inserted at the end of Conde's History of the Domination of the Arabs, and the story itself embodied in the form of an episode in the Diana of Montemayor. From these sources I have drawn it forth, and endeavoured to shape it according to my recollection of the version of the beautiful minstrel; but, alas! what can supply the want of that voice, that look, that form, that action, which gave magical effect to her chant, and held every one rapt in breathless admiration! Should this mere travesties of her inspired numbers ever meet her eye, in her stately abode at Granada, may it meet with that indulgence which belongs to her benignant nature. Happy should I be, if it could awaken in her bosom one kind recollection of the lonely stranger and sojourner, for whose gratification she did not think it beneath her to exert those fascinating powers which were the delight of brilliant circles; and who will ever recall with enthusiasm the happy evening passed in listening to her strains, in the moon-lit halls of the Alhambra.

Rip Van Winkle and other writings

www.ingramcontent.com/pod-product-compliance
Lightning Source LLC
Chambersburg PA
CBHW030257070526
44654CB00045B/1061

* 9 7 8 9 3 9 5 3 4 6 7 3 3 *